I would like to dedicate this book with all my love to my husband, Charlie, for everything he does for me. I also dedicate it to my entire world: Claire, David, James, Lisa, Eden, Lomand, Sawyer, and Millie. I love you all.

Hilary lives with her husband on the outskirts of the beautiful, sparkling granite city of Aberdeen.

She is a retired nurse and has two grown children, four grandchildren, and a one-year-old puppy named Fletcher.

Since retiring, writing has become her passion. Some of her other hobbies include crafting, card-making, socializing with family and friends, and participating in music quizzes.

Hilary Ewen

MR MEEKS AND THE FAMILY BUBBLE

AUSTIN MACAULEY PUBLISHERS™

LONDON • CAMBRIDGE • NEW YORK • SHARJAH

A CIP catalogue record for this title is available from the British Library.

ISBN 9781398476615 (Paperback)
ISBN 9781398476622 (ePub e-book)

www.austinmacauley.com

First Published 2023
Austin Macauley Publishers Ltd®
1 Canada Square
Canary Wharf
London
E14 5AA

Lesley, Allan and their families, xxx

Denise and Debbie, who have always believed and
encouraged me. xxx

Lastly, I would like to thank Austin Macauley Publishers for
all their help.

It's 5:45 am on any given day. The kitchen table is laid for breakfast: the kettle, with just enough water to fill the teapot, stands to attention anticipating the gentle tap of its switch to initiate boiling; the teapot armed with two teabags, ready and eager to fulfil their potential; 50 gm of porridge oats in the saucepan; the milk in a measuring jug, 250ml and not a drop more, being kept cool in the fridge. This preparation would lead us to believe time is of the essence and forward planning is essential for this person.

At 6 am, the alarm clock springs into action, its two giant bells dancing on its head, ringing out in shrill fashion: "It's time to get up!"

Mr Meeks appeared in the kitchen. He pulled his dressing gown cord tight and tied a single bow. A touch of the On switch and the kettle burst into action, milk stirred into the oats swishing around the pan, a burst of flame as the gas ignites.

Water now boiled poured into the teapot, Mr Meeks replaced the lid and slipped over the old knitted green and yellow tea cosy. A fond memory of his mother crossed his mind. He wondered at how many times she must have done the very same thing in her lifetime. Once sat at the table, the urgency of time appears to dissipate.

At 7:30, Mr Meeks put the last of the breakfast dishes away and spritely climbed the stairs again. He surveyed his choice of clothes. Today was different from most; he had to attend a meeting at the solicitor's office in town. He was not particularly looking forward to it, but it had to be done.

Once showered, he dressed. He had chosen his grey suit, white shirt and sky blue tie. His leather shoes still creaked due to lack of use but shined and sparkled like priceless diamonds.

Almost ready to go, he stood at the coat stand, deliberating: would his anorak be smart enough or should he wear his funeral coat? He glanced in the full-length mirror and decided to wear the coat. One last check in the mirror, he nodded, satisfied with the reflection.

Concerned about parking in town, he decided to take the bus. One last check of the house, briefcase in hand, and he was on his way.

Mr Meeks checked his watch; the bus was now two minutes late. He shook his head in disappointment; no one seemed to worry about promptness nowadays. He could see the bus in the distance, plodding along. He was going to speak to the driver and ask why he was late. However, doing the gentlemanly thing, he allowed a woman waiting at the bus stop to go before him. He then witnessed the very reason why the bus was probably late: people. People being unprepared. Because despite having stood at the bus stop for a full five minutes, this lady did not have her money ready or her Old Age Bus Pass to hand and had to rake in her enormous handbag for both. He then felt a pang of sympathy for the driver and understood this particular occupation would require a degree of understanding and patience.

Arriving in town early, Mr Meeks went to look around the Art Centre. He had not been to the Art Centre for some time. He would try to visit at least once or twice a year; he was always trying to expand his knowledge and understanding. However, he was not embarrassed to admit that he struggled to understand modern art.

He slowly walked around taking in the images and trying his best to make sense of them. An artist hanging his painting entitled *Modern Day Stress* observed Mr Meeks staring at his work with a quizzical look. He asked if he could be of any help.

Mr Meeks thought for a moment. "I would be grateful if you could explain to me what YOU see."

The artist explained, "The centre of the painting reflected stress, anger and rage, but as the mind is treated to understanding, relaxation and mindfulness, those feelings are resolved; the outer part emulates harmony, serenity and calm."

Looking satisfied and even pleased, he replied, "Thank you, young man. You explained that very well, and I applaud you for your interpretation, and what's more, I approve and appreciate it."

The artist thanked him, and Mr Meeks went on is way muttering, "Extraordinary!"

Realising the time, Mr Meeks quickened his step. When he arrived at the solicitor's office, the receptionist showed him through.

The "other" Mr Meeks, his brother Edward, was already there. The brothers made no attempt to greet or acknowledge one another.

The solicitor addressed them both: "Nigel, Edward, I would like to begin with a general recap of the situation."

Mr Meeks interrupted, "Please address me as Mr Meeks. I think under the circumstances, it's more appropriate."

The solicitor said, "Sorry I thought it would be easier, as we have two Mr Meeks with us today."

Edward spoke up, "Call me Edward and him the pretentious old fool he is. I warned you about him and his grandiose ways!"

Mr Meeks reached into his briefcase and pulled out a roll of paper, slamming it on the desk. He said, "This should prevent the need for any further dialogue."

The other two men looked stunned. They were not expecting this.

Mr Meeks continued, "This is a plan of the layout of the house, the house my brother would have me sell, reneging on a promise made many years ago that the house would be left to me, as I sacrificed having a life to care for our parents." He rolled out the piece of paper on the desk. "I have thought this over, and if he wants half the house, half the house he can have."

Laying the plans on the table, he continued, "These plans detail which half of the house I will continue to live in and the other half is his. Please inform the other Mr Meeks this is my one and only offer. I bid you both farewell!"

Mr Meeks muttered to himself all the way back to the bus stop. He was so angry – angry at Edward, for making the claim on the property, angry at the solicitor for entertaining his ludicrous claim, but most of all at himself for letting his brother get to him.

Mr Meeks arrived at the bus stop but at the last minute spotted his next door neighbour, Mrs Forbes-Brown. He could not face being interrogated by her. He continued walking past the bus stop. The idea was to have a look around the shops until the next bus was due. However, it began to rain, and with one look to the sky, he confirmed to himself this was most likely not a passing shower.

The thought of traipsing around in the rain visiting shops, especially as he didn't need anything, was not appealing. He decided to treat himself to a half pint of beer in one of the pubs off the main street. It was 4:36. He knew there was a bus at 5:16. He would aim to get that one.

At 11 pm, in other words, closing time, after several pints of beer and some whiskey chasers, Mr Meeks made his way outside. Initially he stood up at the bus stop, until a young lad heading home after a night's work in Burger King passed and said, "No buses at this time of night. old timer." Mr Meeks looked at his watch, struggling to focus, when finally did he realise it was nearly half past eleven. He began to walk towards home, feeling the walk would probably do him good.

Mr Meeks was walking fairly slowly, staring at the ground to ensure each foot did as it should, when he heard this noise which drew his attention away from his feet: a young girl stood alone by the harbour wall crying.

Unable to walk past a damsel in distress, he and his alcohol consumption giving him a false bravery, keeping his distance, not to cause her any further distress, he shouted, "Excuse me, Miss, are you okay?"

Amidst her sobs, she shouted back, "Yes thank you, and may I say you are very kind to ask."

He continued, "Well, if you don't mind me saying, you do not look or sound okay."

She began to sob louder as one often does when being given sympathy.

Mr Meeks made his way closer to her but far enough away as not to scare her. "Can I do anything to help? Do you need money for a taxi or something?"

She began to cry even harder. "That is so nice of you, but to be honest, I have nowhere to go."

Mr Meeks said, "Should you not be going home at this late hour?"

By this time Mr Meeks had made his way closer to her and realised she looked even younger than he initially thought.

"I can't," she said through her tears. "My mum has thrown me out, and I don't know what to do."

Mr Meeks, normally most definitely not known for any type of impulsive behaviour, found himself saying, "Why don't you come back with me and we will see what we can come up with. We will make a pot of tea. Everything is better with a cup of tea."

Mr Meeks even surprised himself. Those were not the words that had been in his head, but his mouth appeared to have a mind of its own tonight.

She nodded.

They began to walk, but Mr Meeks saw a taxi approaching and put his hand out to stop it. They both got in, and Mr Meeks gave the address. They continued the rest of the journey in silence.

Once at their destination, Mr Meeks remained in the car to pay the driver. He handed over the money with a £2 tip, also very unlike Mr Meeks – he felt no one should ever be tipped for a job they are paid for.

The taxi driver said, "Thanks mate." He gesticulated towards the young girl and continued with a wink, "You enjoy yourself, pal."

Mr Meeks was absolutely horrified. He snatched back his £2 coin and got out and slammed shut the door.

Only then did Mr Meeks have a proper look at this young girl. He began to panic a little and had to remind himself how upset she had been.

Once inside, he turned on the heating and went to put on the kettle. While in the kitchen, he was trying to plan his next move. He decided honesty is always best.

He went back into the lounge and said, "Would I be right in thinking you are a lady of the night?"

She said, "I'm not sure what you mean."

"A prostitute?" He shook his head, startled and not quite believing what just came out of his mouth.

But to his complete and utter surprise she said, "Yes, I am!"

He was a little frightened to open his mouth further as he did not appear to be in charge of what was coming out of it. He did his utmost not to appear judgemental or disgusted. "I hope you understand that is not the reason I invited you are here tonight."

She looked up at him from the sofa, and what he saw was not a hardened sex worker but a young girl in pain.

She said, "Oh no, I understand that you are a nice man who saw a girl upset and on her own, and you have been caring enough to help."

Mr Meeks smiled and nodded. He was so glad they appeared to be on the same page.

He went back to the kitchen and continued with the tea making and also put a couple of slices of bread in to toast. When he came back, the girl had fallen asleep. He covered her with a blanket and went to bed.

Next morning Mr Meeks woke and immediately put his hand to his head. The sunlight streaming in the bedroom window told him not only had he had slept in, but he hadn't prepared properly the night before: no blinds shut, he wasn't even changed out of his clothes. He shielded his eyes against the blazing sun bursting through his window; it was hurting his head. He then came to the conclusion it wasn't the light that was the issue; it was the large amount of alcohol he had consumed yesterday. He decided a cup of tea was in order, then he would proceed with the day. He would be no use to anyone until after his first cup of tea.

He swung his legs out of bed and headed to the bathroom. He turned the shower on and stepped in. He was in the process of chastising himself for drinking so much when all of a sudden he remembered the girl. He dried himself and very quickly got dressed in whatever came to hand. He hurried downstairs and peeked into the lounge. She was still in the same position and still sound asleep.

Mr Meeks was a little thrown off this morning as there had been no breakfast prep the night before. He filled the kettle and put the teabags in the teapot. He didn't bother with his porridge this morning. He put bread in the toaster.

He heard a little tap at the kitchen door, and the girl said, "May I use your bathroom?"

Mr Meeks directed her. When she returned, she had washed all the makeup off and had put her hair up in a high ponytail. She looked so young.

Mr Meeks said, "Would you like some tea and toast?"

"Yes, please, and then I will get out of your way," she replied.

While they were both sitting at the table, Mr Meeks, not normally one for chitchat, said, "What are you going to do about somewhere to stay? Can this argument not be fixed with your mother?"

She thought for a minute. "No, I don't think so. My mum remarried, and he is not keen on having me around. I have no clue as to what I am going to do."

Mr Meeks said, "May I ask your age, young lady?"

She smiled. "Yes, of course. I am seventeen."

"Your mother has no business ejecting you from the family home, but then I presume you are not happy to remain there with them making life difficult for you."

She said, "I have to own up to something. I told you a lie last night. You asked me if I was a prostitute, and I said yes. Well, technically I haven't started that job as yet, but it's the only way I can make money fast. I am terrified of sleeping rough on the street and even more terrified of having to have sex." She began to get upset again.

Mr Meeks said, "Your mother should be ashamed of herself. You are no more than a baby. Please eat your breakfast, and when you are ready, we will discuss your next move."

Mr Meeks poured himself another cup of tea. He went to the cupboard searching for some paracetamol. He found a pack. It looked fairly old and dog-eared, so he quickly checked they were in date. He rarely had to succumb to taking pain relief and rarely suffered from headaches. The part of his subconscious that would not normally allow him to become so out of control said, *This is not a headache, you old fool. This is a hangover.*

Mr Meeks went to his wardrobe to see if there was anything he could give this young girl to wear to get her out of that cheap looking short skirt and low-cut top.

He remembered getting a tracksuit from his mother for Christmas. This was of course after she was diagnosed with dementia. Mr Meeks had never in his life been the tracksuit wearing type, but he was also not the type of person who would throw things away either. He had been going to take it to the charity shop, but it was after all one if the last gifts his mother gave him.

He came downstairs and offered it to her. She gratefully accepted, and armed with this and some fresh towels, she went for a shower.

When she came back downstairs, Mr Meeks was on his computer in the lounge. He had been investigating what was available for people who find themselves homeless.

He said, "It would appear we need to make a visit to the council offices. We will do that once we have had our elevenses."

She said, "I'm sorry I never asked your name. I'm Anna, Anna Ward."

Mr Meeks smiled. "I am Mr Meeks. Nice to make your acquaintance, Miss Ward."

She said, "Please call me Anna."

He smiled. "I think Miss Ward is more appropriate."

She smiled and nodded.

Once ready to go, they had just set one foot out of the door when Mrs Forbes-Brown made an appearance. "Good morning, Mr Meeks. Oh, who is this young lady?"

"Good morning, Mrs Forbes-Brown. How are you?"

She said, "I am fine, thank you for asking. Are you not going to introduce me?"

Mr Meeks sighed. "Of course. This is my niece Anna."

Mrs Forbes-Brown said, "So you will be Edward's girl then?"

Anna said, "Yes, that's right, pleased to meet you," as they shook hands.

When they were a decent way away from Mrs Forbes-Brown, Mr Meeks said, "I am sorry about that, Miss Ward. She is a vile woman, so nosey and such a gossip. She is now on husband number 3. I have often wondered what happened to the other two, buried in the cellar no doubt."

Anna laughed. She got the sense that Mr Meeks did not often make jokes – he seemed a very serious person – but that made her giggle.

Once they arrived at the council offices, Mr Meeks explained to the receptionist why they were there. She asked them to take a seat and said someone would call on them, and she gave them a number to respond to when it was called out. They were directed to sit in the blue chairs. The number they had been given was 23; they were currently on 19.

Mr Meeks said, "It shouldn't be too long."

A woman called, "Number 23, please"

Mr Meeks and Anna stood and walked towards the woman. She introduced herself has Fiona and showed them into a very small room that had a desk and three chairs.

Once seated, she asked how she could be of help.

Anna explained, and sensing that it would not look very proper for either of them that she went home with Mr Meeks, a stranger, last night, she said she knew Mr Meeks from the church. To be fair, Fiona did not seem in the least bit interested in how they knew each other. She explained that she would go on the list for allocation but that that may take a while.

Mr Meeks said, "What about now? She needs somewhere for tonight?"

Fiona gave them a list of shelters and explained it was first come first served and to go straightaway to register in one of them.

Having managed to register in one of the hostels, Mr Meeks asked Anna where all her belongings were. She said she did not have any as she was thrown out as she was and had not been allowed back in. She had tried a couple of times but the locks had been changed. All she had was the clothes she was wearing and the personal items in her handbag.

Mr Meeks said, "I am going to head home as I am expecting a builder to come today." He gave her some money and said, "Buy yourself all you can with this."

She said she could not take his money, but he replied, "Let's make it a loan. You can pay me back when you earn yourself your first million." She laughed and thanked him.

Mr Meeks returned home a little flustered. He was not used to being thrown out of his routine. He came into the house and opened a window. The room stank of a stale beer cellar. He silently chastised himself again for drinking so much the day before. He went into the kitchen, and as he as washing up the breakfast dishes, he once again had cause to chastise himself. What had been thinking taking that young girl home with him? He suddenly had an awful thought, if anyone had seen him, they may have reported him to the police. In fact, they would have been right to.

A sharp heavy knock on the door made him physically jump. He tentatively made his way to the door. Following the path of his recent thoughts, he was expecting it to be the police.

Deciding at that moment he would just give himself up, he had no excuse, he was therefore surprised when he opened the door and a man in work trousers and a padded tartan shirt stood in front of him.

The man said, "Hi, I'm Bob."

Mr Meeks must have looked confused as he stared at this tartan clad, rather dirty looking man stood before him.

He repeated, "Bob, the builder, you were expecting me?"

Mr Meeks looked at him suspiciously and repeated, "Bob, the builder?"

Bob checked his paperwork. "Mr Meeks?" he questioned.

"Yes, sorry, I am he, please come in. Excuse my manners, I have had a very strange 24 hours."

Collecting his thoughts, he explained what he wanted done with the property and presented the plans the architect had drawn up.

Bob said, "Good idea making some money by selling off part of this big house. It's too big for one person."

Mr Meeks said, "Oh, I'm not selling. My brother is coming to stay, and quite frankly, the thought of sharing a house fills me with dread. Quite frankly, he is an unscrupulous imbecile."

Bob laughed.

Mr Meeks looked at him not really understanding why he was laughing. "No, I mean it. He is a detestable human being."

Bob said, "Can I ask then why you have decided to live together if you don't get on?"

Mr Meeks said, "Because he is trying to get me to sell this house, and is mistakenly under the impression he owns half. So I told him he can have half, but under no circumstances will I sell my half. There was a gentleman's agreement many years ago that if I remained at home to care for our parents that the house would be mine. He is now disputing this."

Bob, realising that this had clearly been a bone of contention between the brothers, said, "Right you are. I will be in contact with a price and you can let me know if you accept my bid."

Mr Meeks looked disappointed. He said, "Oh is there no way you would be able to tell me today? I would like the work to begin as soon as possible."

Bob replied, "You should really be getting estimates from other people before settling on one!"

Mr Meeks said, "You look honest enough, and you clearly work because your clothes, well, they tell a story."

Bob laughed and brushed a little dust off his jacket.

Mr Meeks said, "Why don't you come into the kitchen? I will make a pot of tea, and you can do your sums."

Bob nodded and followed Mr Meeks. As he went to sit down, Mr Meek said, "I hope you don't take offence but can I just—" he moved past Bob and put a newspaper over the seat.

At this point, Bob wondered how Mr Meeks was going to cope with the building work and knew he was going to have to be especially careful to limit the disruption.

Mr Meeks busied himself with making the tea and put an extra teabag in the pot as he had heard builders like their tea strong. He put out some biscuits, filled the milk jug and put the sugar bowl on the table. He was going to put out the china cups as he usually did for visitors, but he looked at the size of Bob's hands and decided the mugs would be more appropriate in this instance.

He put the teapot on the table and sat down to join Bob. Bob was furiously scribbling away on a piece of paper with a pencil he retrieved from behind his ear. It was the smallest pencil Mr Meeks had ever seen; it had certainly been hard worked in its time.

He finally looked up, and Mr Meeks poured the tea. "Please help yourself to milk and sugar – oh and of course a biscuit."

Bob said, "These are only rough figures but…" he began to explain costings.

Mr Meeks interrupted, "Sorry, that's a lovely array of figures, but the only important thing to me is, when can you start? I thought that was what you were figuring out."

Bob said, "You not concerned about the cost?"

Mr Meeks said, "No, I just need it done quickly. I can hardly stand the thought of that man being my next door neighbour let alone share a house with him, so the sooner it's done, the sooner I can relax knowing I do not have to suffer him under my roof."

Bob said, "I am in the last week of a build. I don't like to take on too much in case of holdups, but this build just needs the finishing touches, so basically I can be all yours from next week."

Mr Meeks smiled. "Excellent! Now, do I need to do anything?"

"Apart from picking what types of doors you want."

Mr Meeks said, "For his side of the house, the cheapest you have; however, I will pick anything required for my side."

Bob said, "Okay, understood."

When Bob left, Mr Meeks felt pleased with himself for getting the ball rolling.

He was washing up the cups when he heard another knock at the door. His heart sank again fully expecting the boys in blue to escort him out in handcuffs.

He took a deep breath and went to the door. It was Anna Ward beaming from ear to ear holding two bulging shopping bags.

She brushed past him. "I thought I would come and let you see what I have bought."

Mr Meeks quickly closed the door. "Ms Ward, you really shouldn't come here without a chaperone. It does not look good on either your character or mine for that matter that we are in a house together alone."

She was barely listening to him. She trailed out her clothes and held each item up for him to see. He was actually pleasantly pleased with what she had bought. She had gone for the sensible – often very pink, but sensible.

She sat down. "I have another surprise for you!"

Mr Meeks was afraid to ask.

"I have enrolled in a college course."

"That is good news, young lady. May I ask what the course is?"

"Access to journalism."

"My goodness, that is good," he said smiling. "None of that gutter press now."

She said, "No, I want to be a serious writer. Anyway, I should go and let you get on. I have to be at the hostel soon to confirm my place for the night."

Off she went like a welcome summer breeze, a spring in her step and a smile on her face.

Mr Meeks called the council to see what was happening with the house allocation for Anna. He would have to keep on top of that. She had been making great strides herself so the least he could do would be to take on the challenge of the establishment and basically annoy them until they gave in and offered something. It would make such a difference to her if she could have somewhere to call her own.

As he sat at the kitchen table, his mind wandered back to the renovation. He was so angry at having to do this. This was not the agreement, and Edward knew this full well. Mr Meeks wandered around then house and decided to start moving the better pieces of furniture to his side of the house, leaving all the things he didn't want in Edward's side.

He really wasn't looking forward to Edward moving in, but he was adamant he was not selling. He had enough money in the bank to pay Edward off but wouldn't give him the satisfaction of that.

After moving several pieces of furniture, he went to sit down at the kitchen table. He put the kettle on and washed out the teapot. He tried to stop thinking about the Edward situation as it always wound him up and left him feeling angry and out of sorts. He checked the fridge and kitchen cupboards to survey what food he had in there for supper. He opened the fridge which had very little in it. Everything seemed very out of sorts. He decided on two soft boiled eggs and toast. Once finished, he declared that to be one of his favourite meals and something he usually associated with breakfast but it was a nice change to have for his evening meal

Mr Meeks retired to the sitting room after his meal. He had music playing and was about to enjoy a glass of sherry when there was once again a sharp knock on the door. Mr Meeks sighed. "Who can this be now?" On his way to answer the door, he thought he may invest in a doorbell – something with a softer tone – if these interruptions were going to continue.

He opened the door and came face to face with Edward. Edward pushed his way past Mr Meeks and went into the lounge. Mr Meeks was alarmed as he realised that Edward was holding two suitcases. Edward dropped his bags on the floor and flopped onto the sofa. Mr Meeks was horrified.

"What, may I ask, do you think you are doing?"

"Come to claim my half of the house, dear brother."

Mr Meeks said, "No, no, no, this is not happening. You cannot come and live here until the property has been prepared."

"What the hell do you mean 'prepared'?" Edward said as he slipped off his jacket.

"No, no, do not make yourself comfortable. You are not living here until the house is completely divided in two. I cannot live with the likes of you."

"Nigel, I have nowhere else to go. Have a heart!" Edward replied.

Mr Meeks, shook his head, picked up Edward's bags and put them outside the front door.

Edward said, "Look, come and sit down. I didn't want to have to tell you this, but I can see I have no option. I have cancer. There is nothing that can be done, and I just want to spend my last couple of months in comfort living with my brother. Is that too much to ask? Have a heart."

Mr Meeks stopped in his tracks. "What are you taking about? Who said you have cancer?"

As Mr Meeks took the bags back inside to the hallway, Edward continued, "I have known for a couple of months. I didn't want you to feel sorry for me and feel compelled to offer me somewhere to stay, but I do want to spend time with my little brother, while I still can."

Mr Meeks was not used to having to make allowances for other people; he was no good at compromise. He was bitter. He had given up enough of his life looking after his parents with little or no help from his brother, but now his brother needed him. Would he be able to walk away, wash his hands of his brother? No, of course not.

From that moment on, he became his brother's keeper, his carer and his dogsbody!

Anna continued to visit regularly. She had no time for Edward; she didn't believe he was ill and felt he was taking advantage of Mr Meeks.

She had had many conversations with Mr Meeks about this and questioned the validity of Edward's claims. Why did Edward not have any hospital or doctor appointments? Why was he not on any medication? Why was his condition not getting any worse?

Mr Meeks said, "Not even my brother would stoop so low as to lie about having cancer." But he had been asking the same questions himself but dismissed the thoughts quickly as he could not conceive that Edward would do such a thing.

The bell Mr Meeks had had installed rang fairly early one morning, and Mr Meeks answered the door to a young man he did not recognise.

"Can I help you?" Mr Meeks asked politely.

"It's me, Uncle Nigel, Ringo."

Mr Meeks looked bewildered. He continued, "I am very sorry, have I made your acquaintance?"

"I am Edward's son. I met you the day Dad moved in."

Mr Meeks stared, eyes wide in complete disbelief. "You are Edward's son? I thought you were from a removal company, and well, you weren't dressed like this either."

Ringo was dressed in a pair of skin tight pink jeans and orange fluffy jumper, yellow Dr Martens boots and was also sporting a very sparkly bum bag.

"Can I come in, Uncle Nigel?"

Mr Meeks stood to one side. "I'm sorry. Of course, please do. Your dad is not up yet."

Ringo said, "I will go and waken him. It's past 10 am. He should be up."

Mr Meeks said, "You should let him sleep, unless your visit is urgent." He continued, "I hope you don't mind and me asking, is Ringo your real name, the one you were born with? And I'm not sure how to say this, you know, I don't know which word is the right one to use now. I don't know what is 'hip'."

Ringo said, "I think from now on, Uncle, we should agree that you never use the word 'hip' in any sentence ever again unless you are talking about the area below your waist, and yes, it's my real name. What was the other question?"

Mr Meeks looked flustered. "I wondered if you were one of the happy people?"

Now it was Ringo's turn to look bewildered. He thought for a few minutes. "Oh you mean gay, am I gay?" He laughed because sometimes being gay had not been so happy for him or hundreds of other people.

Ringo said, "I don't really like giving human beings a label. Have I ever had sex with a man? No. Have I ever had sex with a woman? No. So I'm not sure what you would pigeon-home me as."

Mr Meeks said, "Hole!"

Ringo said, "I am not sure what you are asking me now, so I am going to politely decline"

"Good gracious, it is pigeonhole not home, and I am only asking so as I know how to refer to you," said an exasperated Mr Meeks.

Ringo said, "What's your deal then? Are you one of the happy people?"

"Well, you are your father's offspring?" hailed a belligerent Mr Meeks.

The lounge door opened at that moment, and Edward walked in. It was now almost 11 am.

Edward looked at Ringo and said, "I thought I heard voices. What do you want?"

Ringo said, "I want to know why you are still in bed and Uncle Nigel is doing all the housework?"

Mr Meeks said, "That's okay. I don't want him to tire himself out doing tasks I can undertake."

"Why?" Ringo enquired.

Edward put his hand to his head and lay back on the sofa. Mr Meeks ushered Ringo out the room.

"Ringo, your dad is very unwell. We all need to support him."

Ringo started to laugh. "Please tell me he hasn't used the old cancer trick on you? Uncle Nigel, there is nothing wrong with him. He has used this trick on several wives and girlfriends. It allows him to be lazy and offers him the luxury of doing what he does best – nothing."

Mr Meeks, was horrified. "No, that can't be right. He lost his hair."

Ringo said, "Did he lose it or shave it off?"

Mr Meeks recounted the conversation: *"I am just going to shave my head so that I don't have hair falling out all over the place."*

Mr Meeks asked, "Where was your father living before he came here?"

Ringo said, "With Maggie Brown."

Maggie Brown was the owner of the pub. She lived above the pub. Maggie and her husband, Harry, bought the pub when they were in their twenties and still ran it as a family concern. Harry unfortunately died a couple of years ago. He had a brain tumour. They operated but it reoccurred within months.

Mr Meeks asked, "Was he in a relationship with Maggie?"

"No, I think he would have liked that, but she only put him up because he had nowhere to go," Ringo replied.

Mr Meeks pondered over that for a moment. "So who is living in your father's house then?"

Ringo said, "Has he not explained all this to you?"

"No, we have barely spoken. If it wasn't for the cancer, I wouldn't have allowed him the house."

Ringo said, "I can almost guarantee that he does not have cancer and is not ill. He has used this excuse before; and

Uncle Nigel, he doesn't have a house. He sold the house several years ago and has basically been sofa surfing since."

Mr Meeks said, "You will have to clarify sofa surfing for me, please."

Ringo smiled. "Sorry, he has been basically living in people's spare rooms until they get fed up of him. The reason he is out of Maggie's is that he said he had cancer to guilt her into not throwing him out, and she found out he didn't. After what happened with Harry, who could blame her for being furious."

Edward put on a wounded face. "I wasn't feeling well, and the doctor said it might be cancer or heart failure or something just as serious. My golf clubs are still there."

Mr Meeks shook his head and muttered under his breath, "Despicable man."

"No need to worry about your golf clubs. I will go and pick them up this afternoon."

"Oh, there's no hurry!" Edward added quickly.

"Nonsense! I have to go out anyway. I pass the end of the road."

"I will come with you. We can stay at Maggie's for a couple of pints."

Mr Meeks smiled. "No problem."

The minute Edward left the room to get ready to go out, Mr Meeks put on his coat and asked Ringo if he wanted a lift home.

Ringo knew this was his uncle's way of finding out the truth about Edward from his mother and Maggie.

Ringo's mother wasn't in. He then went to Maggie's. Maggie opened the door.

"Oh my goodness, look who it is. How are you?"

"I am well, Mrs Brown."

Maggie knew Mr Meeks well enough to know he would never call her by her first name, so she didn't bother correcting him.

Maggie made a pot of tea. They sat at one of the tables in the bar. After a short catch-up, Mr Meeks said, "I'm here to pick up the rest of Edward's belongings and to ask you a couple of questions, if that's okay."

Maggie said, "The bag is in the back of the bar, and his golf clubs are in the hall cupboard." She went to get up.

He said, "Don't fuss right now. I will get it on my way out, no hurry for that"

Mr Meeks fidgeted a little as he wasn't sure he was ready to hear the truth but knew he had to.

"So Edward tells me he has cancer. I believe he also told you this, but from what I am told by Ringo this is untrue."

Maggie's face told Mr Meeks all he really needed to know.

She said, "Yes, he did tell me he had cancer but was never very forthcoming with facts. I began to suspect he was lying after about a week or so; he was too happy for a guy who had a limited amount of time left to live. Deep down, I knew it wasn't. I called him on the fact that he didn't appear to be deteriorating, wasn't attending hospital appointments and has never gone to the GP as far as I was aware. He just said, 'Expect you want me to leave then,' and by the time I got home from the shops that day, both him and most of his belongings were gone."

Mr Meeks looked visibly shocked.

She continued, "He was supposed to be here for a few nights which turned into months. He had promised to help out, but that never materialised, and he was helping himself from the bar – not the odd drink or anything but it was a bottle at a time, and I have to account for that. I think I am a generous person, but not once did he put his hand in his pocket or buy as much as a packet of biscuits. When I found out he had lied about the cancer, that was the last straw. After what I went through with Harry, I thought that was extremely insensitive."

Mr Meeks said, "I apologise on behalf of my brother, and I would like to pay for his time here. I can give you a check today or come back with cash."

Maggie said, "You will not. You are already going to have to part with a lot of your cash if he is living with you now, and none of this is your fault."

Mr Meeks said, "We will see. I had plans in motion to split the house in half." He went on to explain all about the plans and she was in complete agreement.

She urged him to get that all written up by a solicitor. "He has several children, some he has never seen. You know what it's like when someone comes knocking at the door in twenty years."

Surprised, Mr Meeks asked, "How many children does he have?"

Maggie laughed. "To be honest, he was never exact about it. I'm not sure he knows. He doesn't even remember their names, and they have nothing to do with him." Maggie continued, "Mr Meeks, before you go, I have had a girl apply for a part-time job, and she put you down as a reference – Anna Ward?"

Mr Meeks aware he was blushing said, "Oh yes, I haven't known her for long, but she has had a hard time and is trying to get her life back together. Why don't you take her on on a trial basis to see how she works out. She is a lovely girl though, a proper survivor."

Mr Meeks was so glad Maggie did not ask him how he knew Anna. What on earth would he say? He dodged that bullet by looking at his watch declaring, "Is that the time already."

Edward was furious that he was left behind. Mr Meeks made up some story about Ringo having to be at work urgently.

At their evening meal that night, Mr Meeks asked Edward if he would be able to go home for a few days so they could get the work done in the house. The builder was starting on Monday. Edward hesitated.

Mr Meeks went on to say, "It's probably best you are not here when they are doing the work anyway. You have a nasty cough already. You don't need to aggravate that further."

Edward went very quiet. "Thing is old boy, I have rented the house out, so it won't be an option."

"Well, what about your flat? You could go back there, couldn't you?"

"What flat are you talking about?"

"The one you bought off the council years ago, on the main street."

"Oh, I don't have that one now. I sold it years ago."

"Oh, right, I was told you rented it out and had been renting it out for some time, must take in a bit of money."

Edward suddenly felt a bit lightheaded. He stood and staggered towards the bedroom. "Sorry, dear brother. I don't feel myself at the moment. I am going to have to lay down. Can you put my plate in the micro?"

The following day, Mr Meeks could hear someone trying to put something through the letterbox. They were struggling, so he went to the door. It was Anna. He surprised himself at how pleased he was to see her.

Mr Meeks said, "Hello, Ms Ward. How are you?"

Anna replied, "I'm well, thank you. I just came by to give you this."

It was a present beautifully wrapped in a blue gingham checked paper with a navy ribbon. Mr Meeks was close to tears. No one had given him a present in a long time.

"There was no need for you to spend your money on me," he said as he carefully peeled off the Sellotape to preserve the paper. Inside was a beautiful blue lambs wool jumper. He was absolutely delighted with it.

Anna said, "I thought it would go with your grey suit."

"It will indeed, but really this is too much."

"It's a thank you for putting a word in for me at the pub. I also have another job; I have a job every weekday from 3 pm to 5 pm in the college library, but I couldn't have done any of it without your support. We both know where I would be right now."

Edward's nose had got the better of him. He appeared in the kitchen. "Hello there, young lady. Hope you are not letting that brother of mine take a loan of you. Hasn't got you darning his socks, has he?"

Anna scowled at him.

"I know he is your brother, Mr Meeks, but he gives me the heebie-jeebies."

Mr Meeks didn't laugh often, but he had a good old chuckle about that.

"I am not at all sure I even know what the heebie-jeebies is, but whatever it is, he is all that and more. However, we should not make fun of people who are ill."

"What's wrong with him?" Anna asked.

"He has cancer; he is dying."

Anna screwed her nose up. "Are you sure that wasn't just a way to wheedle his way in here?" She was so switched on, nothing got past her.

The work began on the renovation of the house. It wasn't going to be a big job, and the builder had a large team of men. Edward, funnily enough, managed to find somewhere to stay for the couple of weeks while it was being done.

Mr Meeks had made up his mind he would try to keep out of Edward's way when he came back. He had no interest in adding further stress to his life, and the best way of doing that was to keep away from Edward. Of course should his "illness" begin to deteriorate, he would do what he could for his brother.

When Edward came back, he got settled into his part of the house and did not bother Mr Meeks at all, which was very surprising. He appeared to spend a lot of his time in the house.

After about eight weeks of no communication from Edward, Mr Meeks thought he should pay him a visit to make sure everything was okay.

Edward took some time to answer. He was still in his pyjamas and looked awful.

"How are you, brother?" Mr Meeks asked.

"To be honest, not great. I have not been able to keep any food down and have been coughing up real mucky stuff."

Mr Meeks could see that Edward appeared to have a fever. "I'm calling the doctor," Mr Meeks said panicked by what he was seeing before him. He continued, "Oh, for goodness sake, Edward, you are clearly unwell."

Edward went to stand to go to the toilet and collapsed on the floor. Mr Meeks dialled 999. Edward was admitted to hospital.

Mr Meeks felt bad for not believing him about the cancer because he clearly was ill.

After initial blood tests were done, they were concerned about the levels of something or the other. They told Mr Meeks they were running some tests to determine what the problem was.

Mr Meeks said, "I thought it may just be a deterioration of the cancer."

The doctor asked, "What cancer?"

"He has been diagnosed with cancer."

"Where?" the doctor asked.

"You know I am not sure; he never said. I would take a guess at lungs because he smokes those dreadful roll-ups and has since about the age of 13."

The doctor said, "Sorry, I meant where did he receive this diagnosis?"

"Here," Mr Meeks replied.

The doctor scratched his head. "There is nothing in his notes. Do you happen to know when this was diagnosed?"

Mr Meeks, now scratching his head, said, "No, I am sorry, young man. I have not been privilege to that information."

"There is nothing in the notes about it. I will speak to the secretaries and see if they can have a look."

Mr Meeks knew now that the story about the cancer was most likely untrue. He knew Edward was capable of stooping that low, but had once again given him the benefit of the doubt.

Later that day the doctor came to speak to Mr Meeks. Mr Meeks was still sitting by the bedside. Edward had not woken. Edward had put Mr Meeks down as his next of kin. The doctor asked if he could speak to Mr Meeks in the relatives' room. Mr Meeks followed the doctor.

Once seated, the doctor said, "There is never an easy way to say this, but your brother does most likely have lung cancer, and we suspect it has metastasised to the liver and brain."

Mr Meeks said, "So he did have cancer all along. I was so sure he was putting it on."

The doctor said, "There is no evidence that your brother has been to the hospital for any appointments for several years, so in answer to your concerns, there is no evidence that he has already been given a diagnosis. Life appears to have played a cruel trick on him."

The doctor explained that they were unsure if Edward would wake again. "We have ordered a head CT scan as we think he may have had a bleed."

Mr Meeks got a little flustered. "Edward has a few ex-wives and even more children, but I only know one of them, and I would not know how to contact any of them."

"That's okay. We will see if the ward admin girls can come up with something, but we will know more after the scan."

The doctor headed off to ensure the request for the urgent scan had been done.

Mr Meeks wasn't sure what he should do; should he stay there or go home? He hadn't planned to be out so long, and he couldn't remember what kind of state he had left the house in. He was jolted out of that particular worry by his mobile phone ringing.

It was Anna. She said, "I just wondered if you were okay. I got to the house and there was no sign of you. I looked through the window and the breakfast dishes have not been done."

He thought to himself, *What a clever girl.* "Just use your key and go in and make sure everything is okay."

She said, "I don't like going in when you are not there."

"Please do, Ms Ward. It would put my mind at rest and then I could remain here."

"Where are you?" Anna asked.

"I'm at the hospital. Edward has taken unwell. Stay there and I will be home within the hour, or if not, I will call"

Anna said, "I'm sorry to hear that. Is there anything you need?"

"No, I appreciate you asking, but I think I have all I need."

As Mr Meeks finished his call, the porters had come to collect Edward for his scan. Once he had gone, Mr Meeks was thinking what a disorderly mess everything was. He had no knowledge of Edward's wishes, no knowledge of how to contact his wives and children; however, Paul may be the lynchpin there.

Edward was returned to the ward and made comfortable again by the nurses. They told Mr Meeks the doctors wanted to speak with him before he left for home. He went back to the lounge and poured himself some water.

Half an hour later, the doctors appeared in the relatives' room. The doctor motioned for Mr Meeks to sit down. He knew before the doctor spoke, who could tell by the look on his face. "I am terribly sorry to inform you that your brother is what we would call brain-dead. It is only the machines that are keeping him alive. We did the test then repeated it with the same outcome."

Mr Meeks thanked him and went back to sit with Edward for a while. He asked the nurse when they would think about switching off the machines. She asked about organ transplant. Mr Meeks explained that they had not had that conversation but wondered due to the cancer if anything was viable. He advised them he would return home and try to contact someone in Edward's family. They said nothing would be done that day so not to worry too much.

Mr Meeks travelled home. He couldn't believe what had happened. When he arrived, he found the house lit and warm and a beautiful smell of dinner cooking.

Anna popped out of the kitchen. "I hope you don't mind; I thought you might be hungry when you came home. How is Edward?"

Mr Meeks plumped down on his chair. "I am afraid Edward will not recover. He is brain-dead, meaning the machines are the only thing keeping him alive."

"I am so sorry, I can't believe it. He didn't look unwell at all. Good job he made up that book."

Mr Meeks said, "What book?"

"I was completing my application for college and it asked for a next of kin. I don't have anyone; I meant to ask but I have put you. Anyhow Edward was saying that he didn't have a will and no one would know who to contact or what his wishes were. A couple of weeks later, he said he had his little black book completed and winked."

Mr Meeks went to Edward's room and looked in his bedside drawer, and lo and behold, a little black book with a sticker on the front saying, *"In the event of my death."*

Mr Meeks said, "I have no wish to read it but need the contact details, would you please." Handing the notebook to Anna, he sat poised with his own notebook ready to write down the numbers.

Anna found the numbers and passed them on. She continued reading as he had put down his wishes for his funeral,

"A modest casket. Cremation, no flowers, no church horse-shit. There is little money to offer anyone as most of the people at the funeral have already bled me dry. The half of the house I stole from my brother should be returned to him with my sincere apologies. Oh, and no hymns – I think it should be one of my favourite songs, My Ding-a-Ling, Chuck Berry. Okay, that was a joke; can someone pick Nigel up off the floor? Seriously, Bridge over Troubled Water, Simon and Garfunkel.

Apologies to those who feel they require them. Thanks to those who were kind and have forgiven me already, and love and best wishes to all.
Edward"

Mr Meeks contacted Edward's first wife who said she would contact all the kids. Anna was in tears when Mr Meeks went back into the sitting room. He said, "My goodness, what has happened?"

She pointed to the text in the notebook. He read it and smiled.

"We had a complex relationship. I would admit I am not easy to live with, and he could be an extremely pompous and condescending bugger, but at the end of the day, he is my brother, and I love him."

Anna started to put on her jacket.

"Are you leaving?" Mr Meeks said surprised.

"Yes, I don't want to intrude."

"You are not intruding. Please stay for something to eat, and I will give you a lift home on my way back to the hospital."

"Are you sure?" she asked.

"Ms Ward, you know I would never say anything I don't mean; it's just not in my character."

Anna nodded and laughed.

They ate the meal Anna had prepared. Mr Meeks congratulated her saying it was as nice a meal as he had had in a very long time.

They had a cup of tea, and then it was time to go back to the hospital. Mr Meeks was not looking forward to this at all, but it had to be done.

When they arrived at Anna's flat, Mr Meeks stopped outside her building. There were around 8 to 10 people milling around at the front door.

"Who are they?" Mr Meeks asked.

He was quite taken aback by Anna's reply. "Junkie shits."

"Have they caused you any bother?"

"Sometimes, but it's fine. I can look after myself. Take care, I will speak to you soon," she shouted as she was leaving.

Mr Meeks was not at all happy about leaving Anna there, but he also did not want to take her to the hospital – both options appeared traumatising.

Arriving at the hospital, he parked up and headed to the ward. He asked to see the doctor and said that all the family had now been contacted. None of them wanted to visit, to have this as their last memory, but that they were all happy for the machines to be switched off and if any organs viable then to use them. He went in to say his goodbyes. He left with tears rolling down his cheeks.

He could hardly recall any of his journey home. He had meant to drive past Anna's flat to make sure things were okay but was home and in the drive before he knew it. He looked at his mobile; there was no calls or messages from her so he took it all was okay.

Around 2 am, his mobile phone rang. He sat up in bed and looked at the number. He didn't recognise it; he answered tentatively. "Hello."

"Am I speaking to Mr Meeks?"

"You are indeed."

"My name is Michael. I am one of the doctors from A&E. We have a young woman who has been taken in following an assault. She remains unconscious but we found your number as her emergency contact in her phone."

"I will be right there!" Mr Meeks said, jumping out of bed.

Mr Meeks threw on a pair of trousers and a jumper; no time to ensure they looked okay. He just left, leaving the lights on, door locked but uncharacteristically, not checked.

Back at the hospital he left barely six hours ago, he parked in a disabled space and ran in. The receptionist asked him to wait in the waiting room and she would find out what was happening.

The doctor appeared. He held out his hand to greet Mr Meeks.

"Hi, I'm Michael. We spoke on the phone. She has not come round as yet. But her vitals are stable."

"You need to be a little more specific young man, vitals?"

"Sorry, I mean all the tests we would perform to check for any abnormalities all appear to be stable meantime."

Mr Meeks head in hands said, "What on earth happened? I only dropped her at her flat a few hours ago."

"The police may be able to tell you a bit more, but from what I understand, they have the culprit in custody. Now before you go in, I need to warn you she is in a bit if a state. Her face is badly bruised and swollen. Sorry, what relationship are you to Anna?"

"Just a friend, nothing inappropriate, you understand, but I am very fond of her. She is trying to turn her life around with little to no help from anyone. Her mother has thrown her out on the street because she has a new boyfriend to please. Disgusting behaviour."

Michael nodded, "Fine, I will take you to her."

Mr Meeks staggered back at the shock of seeing Anna. Her face was so bruised and swollen, she would struggle to see out her eyes even if she was awake. Her hair had been cut, her lip bust, her nose broken and well, the injuries just go on. Mr Meeks thought it had to be something to do with the boys who were hanging around at the front of her flat. He had already written the strongly worded letter to housing in his head. He nodded off, and woke with a moan from Anna. He stood, and using her first name, he said, "Anna, you are in hospital. You are okay but have been hurt badly. I am going to get the nurse, but I will be right outside."

The nurse came out after about 20 minutes. "You can go back in now, Sir."

"Thank you."

He went in to see Anna propped up in the bed hardly able to see or speak.

Mr Meeks said, "You are going to be okay. Just answer me one question, was this the boys outside your flat?"

Anna shook her head.

"Right, I am going to let you get some rest, but I will be back first thing tomorrow."

Anna nodded. On his way out, he asked the staff to contact him if there was deterioration and asked what the visiting times were the following day.

On his way out of the ward, he passed a woman heading into the ward. She looked familiar but he felt she may be a nurse or live close to him. Seconds later she was running down the corridor after him. No wonder she looked familiar, it was Anna's mother. She asked if she could possibly have a chat. They went to the relatives' room.

Mr Meeks did not sit down. He didn't want to spend time with this woman given what he already knew. She thanked him for looking after her 'little girl'. He was not a violent man and would never strike a woman but he had a fleeting thought at that moment that he would like to punch this despicable idiot. He did, however, think it was decent of her to go to the hospital to see Anna. Little did he know there was an ulterior motive.

Once home, he reflected on his last 12 hours and felt there had never before been a more harrowing time in his life. He felt he would never sleep, but he was so physically exhausted that next thing he knew it was 8 am. His routine was out of kilter. This would normally have made him anxious and panicked, but there were more important things to worry about at the moment. He checked the opening times for John Lewis; he needed to buy some essentials for Anna.

Once at the shop, he spoke to one of the employees and explained the situation.

She said, "I can help with that. If you follow me."

"Young lady would there be any way I could leave this up to you? I would be very uncomfortable walking around in the women's department. I am looking for three night dresses, a pair of slippers, undergarments, a leisure suit and some tops, some toiletries and anything else you can think of."

"Certainly. What type of budget are we looking at, Sir?"

"No budget, Miss; whatever it costs is fine, and please do not stint on quality. I will have a look around the handbags. You can look at the ones I have chosen to ensure they are fitting."

"No problem, Sir"

Around 45 minutes later, she appeared with exactly what he wanted: nightwear, daywear, underwear and slippers. She explained she had also added pumps for when this person had to leave hospital. He showed her the bags. She put them all back and chose a more appropriate one and handed him a bag of toiletries. He handed her his card. He never even asked how much.

He headed straight up to the hospital as he had been told he could visit at any time. He parked and took a slow walk to the entrance.

He could not believe how many people were outside smoking. He felt like telling them that was what killed his brother, but today was not a day for confrontation.

He continued to the ward, stopping to speak to the nurse at the nurses' station. "How is Ms Ward?"

"Much better. She is now in the single room at the end."

"Many thanks," Mr Meeks said, walking purposefully down the ward.

He got to the room and knocked on the door. A familiar but somewhat strained voice shouted, "Come in."

Anna was sitting up in bed, looking much brighter than she had been a few hours earlier. He handed over the bags and bags of shopping. "Some essentials."

Anna opened the bags and began to cry. "Thank you. Thank you so much. I have no idea how I will ever be able to pay you back"

"No payment required. Now, who did this to you?"

Anna laughed. "No messing about with you is there?"

"The perpetrator cannot be allowed to get away with this."

She said now very serious, "Oh, he won't, no matter what anyone says or threatens."

"So you know who it is?"

"I do indeed, and I am waiting for the police to come and interview me anytime now."

Mr Meeks smiled. "Well done! I am so proud of you. Are you going to tell me who it was?"

"Yes, it's no secret. It was my mother's boyfriend. He came to my flat and attacked me. He tried to… well, you know."

"Ms Ward, I would have thought you would know by now that there are many things I do not know, especially about women."

Anna laughed. "Okay, but remember you asked for this. He tried to rape me. He had my knickers off, and although I was fighting him with all the strength I had, he was winning as I was getting tired. However, the boys at the front door heard me screaming, rushed to the flat, pulled him off me and rang the police and ambulance."

Mr Meeks said, "Ah, it was them who called the ambulance?"

The penny dropped with a loud clang as he realised that was the reason her mother was at the hospital and not because she was concerned about Anna. She was trying to get Anna to withdraw charges.

Anna continued, "I need to have an operation on my arm. They are going to schedule it for tomorrow. I won't be able to work until it is healed. Would you be able to contact my work? I have tried to contact them but the mobile signal in here is not great."

"No problem. Please write down anyone you want me to contact, and I will do that when I get home. You will need to ask for a sick line either from the hospital or your GP."

They spent the rest of his visit doing a crossword. The nurse said, when he was leaving, how nice it was to hear her laughing.

Mr Meeks said, "She has asked me to contact her work. Have you any idea of a timescale I can give them?"

The nurse looked at her notes. "She is having to get a metal plate put in. She is going to be very sore for a while, but she will be able to go home soon. She will just need to go to her doctor for her STD results."

Mr Meeks said, "Sorry, STD?"

"Sexually transmitted diseases."

Mr Meeks' face said it all.

The nurse was very apologetic. She said, "I am so sorry. I thought you knew. She said she told you."

He said, "She did, but that doesn't remove the element of shock, I'm afraid."

He left the hospital in tears for the second time in so many days. It would appear what she described as an attempted rape may have gone a little further than she wanted to admit.

When he got into the car, he had a message on his mobile. It was the builders saying they were sorry to hear his bad news and they just wanted to let him know the building work was now finished.

All the way home, he thought about that man busting his way into Anna's flat. She wasn't safe there. He knew then what had to happen. She would move into the other half of the house; she would be safe there. He would discuss it with her in the morning, but he was not taking no for an answer.

The following day, Mr Meeks was listening to *Radio 4,* a political broadcast, when his less invasive doorbell rang. He answered the door to a very well dressed young man who looked very familiar.

"Can I help you?" Mr Meeks asked.

The young man said, "I do hope so, Sir. I am your oldest nephew. My name is Edwin."

"Come in, please."

The reason Mr Meeks thought he knew him was because he was the spitting image of himself – his build, colouring and mannerisms. He was mesmerised.

He said, "I am so sorry, Edwin, I knew nothing of you. Edward was never very forthcoming about his family, his children in particular. Did you know your father well?"

He smiled. "No, I never met him."

Mrs Meeks said, "What do you mean you never met him?"

"He left when my mother was eight months pregnant."

Mr Meeks shook his head. "I'm sorry, I had no idea. Edward and I were not what you could call close. Once he left home, we only saw him sporadically and usually only when he needed something, usually money. Is there anything in particular I can help with?"

"No, not really. I just wanted to meet you. I hope you don't mind?"

"No, not in the slightest. So you are Mary's boy?" Mr Meeks asked.

He laughed. "No, I am Jenny's boy. I think she was the one before Mary."

"Jenny? What was your mother's maiden name?"

"Morris."

Mr Meeks staggered and looked visibly shocked.

"Are you okay, Uncle?"

Catching his breath, he said, "Yes, sorry, would you like some tea?"

Mr Meeks went to the kitchen and leaned against the worktop to steady himself. He could not believe what he was hearing. If Edward was still alive, Mr Meeks would think it was his brother playing yet another cruel joke.

Jenny was Mr Meeks one and only girlfriend. He loved her, but when his parents initially became unwell, he broke off their relationship. He thought it unfair on her as he was sure she would want to have a family of her own but he was committed to caring for his parents. He recalled Edward left very soon after that and they didn't see him for years. None of them had any idea where he had gone, but of all the things Edward had ever done, this was the most unforgivable. Starting a relationship with the one true love of his life and then leaving her when she would have needed him the most and not even mentioning this was completely unforgivable.

Edward had always been jealous of Mr Meeks' relationship with Jenny. She was pretty, intelligent and fun.

Mr Meeks shook his head. He must have followed Jenny when their relationship ended. He couldn't believe he had done this, not to HIS Jenny. He felt all kinds of hate for his brother all over again.

He said to Edwin, "I don't mean to be rude, but I have to go to hospital visiting this evening. But you are more than welcome to stay, and we can have dinner when I get back. I would love to hear more about you."

"Uncle, I would like that. Is there a B&B around here I could book into?"

"Nonsense. If you are all right to stay overnight, you can stay here. I don't have much in the fridge, but I am sure we can make something out of what's there."

Mr Meeks went off to the hospital to visit Anna. She was looking a bit better. She told him her operation was going to be first thing in the morning and she would probably be in hospital for another three to four days.

Mr Meeks said to Anna, "You will never guess who is at my house right now cooking dinner."

"You haven't given into that randy neighbour, have you?"

"Ms Ward, I have not—what neighbour?"

She laughed. "I don't know. Tell me?"

He told Anna the story.

She said, "Are you sure he is for real?"

"Totally! It is like looking at me 20 years ago."

"Are you saying he might be yours?"

"No, not at all. I am just saying there is a family likeness. He never met Edward, Edward walked out when his mother was eight months pregnant."

Anna said, "What a shit-bag"

"Right, I will be back tomorrow."

"I wouldn't bother," Anna said. "They said I will be out of it most of the day. Wait and come the following day."

"Okay, I will call the ward to see how you are, and if you feel better and want a visit, have them call me."

Mr Meeks went home and was so pleased to see the lights on. When he opened the door, immediately, he could smell something very tasty. Before taking off his coat, he went into the lounge. Edwin was reading a book.

"That smells very appetising. I will pop out and get us some wine."

"No need, Uncle, I have already been. I hope you like curry."

"I do indeed."

When they sat down to dinner, Edwin said, "I hope your friend is feeling better."

"She is having an operation on her arm tomorrow. I was wondering, how quickly do you need to get back home? Please say no if it's an imposition, but let me explain first."

He went on to explain how he met Anna, what she had been through and how they met. He showed Edwin his father's instruction on the event of his death and said instead of putting the house back to the way it was, he thought he would ask Anna to move in.

Edwin said, "I think that is a fantastic idea. She is very vulnerable on her own at that age. What was her mother thinking?"

Mr Meeks said, "Well, having now met her mother, I just cannot imagine for the life of me how Anna turned out the decent loving human being she is. And now that she has reported the mother's boyfriend to the police, I would imagine she will never be welcome at home."

"Have you spoken to her about this as yet, Uncle?"

"No, not yet but what I thought was if you are staying around for a few days, you could maybe help with the decor of the other half of the house."

Edwin said immediately, "That would be great fun. Yes, I can do that. I am on holiday this week."

The pair enjoyed their curry, shared a bottle of wine and then had a couple of beers. They watched a John Wayne film then went to bed.

Mr Meeks waited until around 2 pm to call the hospital. The operation has gone well; Anna was still sleeping off the anaesthetic, but the surgeon had been pleased with how well the op had gone.

"Can you tell her I will be in tomorrow to visit, please?"

He passed on the information to Edwin.

"Oh, that is good news. We need to be busy then."

They went to the other half of the house to see what had been done and what needed to be done. Mr Meeks had not been in since it was finished.

They carried the new bed he had bought for one of the spare rooms down to house B. The walls were painted a very modern grey colour, which was fine. They managed to get bedding and other bits and pieces. There was no sofa, however. On the way back to the car, they went past one of those one off designer kind of shops, a hanging chair in the window. Mr Meeks glanced in the window on the way past and then walked back.

"Edwin, this is the very one."

Edwin smiled nodding in agreement.

Mr Meeks said, "Would you like to come with me to visit today. I would really like to introduce you to one another."

"I would like that," Edwin replied.

The men went home, worked on House B for a few hours, showered and went to visit. Anna was sitting on the chair reading when they arrived. When they came in the room, Anna stood to greet them. She had been looking forward to seeing Mr Meeks. They handed over their gifts, flowers, chocolates and a phone charger.

Anna said to Edwin, "This is the reason I love your Uncle so much; I didn't even have to ask for this."

They all laughed.

Mr Meeks said, "I have a suggestion, and please listen before butting in."

She laughed. "Who me? As if."

Mr Meeks explained. Anna remained silent as promised.

Edwin said, "Sounds like a win-win situation. You will be where he can look after you, and you will be where you can look after him, which makes me happy."

Mr Meeks went to get some coffee for everyone. Edwin and Anna chatted. Edwin was the one to finally persuade Anna the house thing was a good idea. She explained that she did not want to appear to be taking a loan of him – there had been enough of that – but she admitted she was a little jumpy about being on her own again after what had happened, and she did feel he also needed some company.

Anna went on to explain to Edwin that his uncle was a special man. He had his "little ways" but he also was very honest and said she could see Edwin had the same kind of issues. He laughed and told her that when his uncle opened the door it was like him fast forwarding 30 years. Even he could see the uncanny resemblance.

Mr Meeks came back into the room struggling with the three coffees. Edwin jumped to his feet to help. Once sitting down enjoying their coffee, Edwin said, "We were chatting, when you were away, about house B."

Mr Meeks said, "Oh right, and what was the outcome of those talks?"

Anna said, "I would like to accept your offer, but there has to be one stipulation: you have to stop calling me Ms Ward. It's Anna."

Mr Meeks said, "I am delighted that you have accepted the offer, ANNA, and my stipulation is that you call me Uncle Nigel and let me treat you as I would if you were my niece."

Anna said, "Well, Uncle Nigel, I would shake on it, if I could."

They all laughed. Things were returning to normal.

Mr Meeks admitted he was surprised at the immediate acceptance of the proposal. He expected much more resistance from "I am Ms Independent" than he got.

While they were chatting, the police came back to ask if they could have a chat.

They said, "If you could excuse us, gentlemen?"

Anna said, "No, it's okay. This is my uncle and my cousin, and they know all about what happened."

"My name is Officer Reynolds, and this is Officer Porter. We wanted to let you now that the perpetrator has been apprehended and is in custody awaiting bail hearing."

Anna said, "Then what happens?"

"We continue our investigation. We are waiting for the results of the physical examination." Officer Reynolds knew by the look on Anna's face she would rather they go no further with that.

"Is he likely to get bail?" Anna asked, clearly terrified of that thought.

Officer Reynolds said, "I can't answer that. In all honesty, it is very difficult to predict. I would hope, however, with the evidence we have, the answer would be no."

Mr Meeks, anger building inside him, said, "He ought to be horsewhipped and chemically castrated."

Anna said, "Uncle Nigel! Geez we have enough to worry about without adding medieval punishments to the scenario."

They all laughed, even Mr Meeks, but inside he was still thinking it would be a good idea.

Two days later and Anna was ready to be discharged, with strict instruction not to use her arm for at least a week but to continue with her daily exercises, and to increase as able. Mr

Meeks and Edwin were both there to collect her. She was surprised and pleased Edwin had not returned home. They were given instructions for all the medication and a return appointment for a further check-up.

They arrived back at the house. They tried to assist Anna out of the car, but she waved them away. She could see this was going to be one of those nightmares where the person deep down is pleased that it's happening.

When shown into house B, she began to cry. No one had ever, ever done anything like this for her before. It was no longer the stark dwelling of an elderly man but of a hip young woman who enjoys the boho lifestyle. Anna especially loved the chair, suspended from high above.

Mr Meeks said, "Now Anna, I think it is rest time." He provided a beautiful patchwork blanket and shut the new blinds.

She lay in the semi-darkness and smiled from ear to ear. She couldn't sleep. She didn't want to, but nevertheless sleep washed over her and encompassed her just as the new patchwork covering had. Next thing she knew, it was an hour and a half later.

When she woke, she was thirsty, and it was almost time to take her medication. Just as that thought left her head, there was a knock in the door.

"Medication time," said Mr Meeks.

Anna sat up and took the medication with a glass of water. She set down the glass on a coaster on her bedside table.

Mr Meeks said, "Excuse me, young lady, more water. It says in the instructions 'to be taken with a full glass of water.'"

She knew there was no point in arguing with him so for once did what she was told.

"That's better. Now Edwin has set up a film for us to watch, so when you are ready, come on through and we will have snacks and be educated by *Mr Bean* or something or other."

Anna smiled knowing exactly why Edwin picked that film. She swung her legs out of bed, her slippers ready and waiting. When she got through to House A, she could hear the two men chatting away.

She shouted, "Hello, I'm here."

They had made a special place for her in front of the television. She sat down with her own plate of snacks, and the film began.

About a quarter way through the film, Anna looked across at her two knights in shining armour and could never remember a time when she felt this happy.

They had an "Interval" about half way through to replenish the snacks and drinks. Before the film started again, Mr Meeks said, "Does Mr Bean remind you of anyone?"

Anna and Edwin burst out laughing.

He continued, "Oh, so you see it too. This film could actually be based on you, Edwin."

Anna laughed even louder.

Edwin wasn't sure, *Was he joking or is that what he really thinks?*

Mr Meeks pointed his finger at him. "Hah, got you!"

Anna had never seen Mr Meeks in such a jovial mood. That was about to take a sharp decline. Fun was extinguished as quickly as the flame being blown out on a candle, with a persistent ring of the doorbell.

Mr Meeks moved quickly to the door to attend to this urgency. When he opened the door, this raging woman pushed past him shouting, "Where the fuck is she?"

She headed to the lounge, Mr Meeks in hot pursuit. Anna was already aware of what was heading her way. She was aware she needed to protect her arm, so moved to the back of the room. Edwin stood in front of her not quite knowing what was happening.

The woman got as close as she could to Anna and began shouting obscenities and pointing her finger.

Mr Meeks was shouting, "Madam, if you do not leave my house right now I will call the police." He had the phone in his hand.

The woman turned her wrath towards Mr Meeks. "What is this sickness you are running here anyway, you old perv!"

Anna dashed out from behind Edwin shouting, "How dare you! How dare you speak to him like that? Now get out!"

The woman said, "You better withdraw your statement with the police or this will not be the last you see of me."

Anna said, "Are you mad? Of course I am not withdrawing my statement. That man raped and beat me. He beat me so hard he broke my arm, and you want me just to let that go? Well, I won't, and if you were any kind of mother you wouldn't want me to."

Her mother replied, "You have always offered it to any man that passed you by."

Anna said, "Jesus! Mother, I was a virgin before all this, and who are you to lecture me on morals. Now get out and do not come back."

Her mother still showing little remorse, turned to leave. "Maybe it's time I left you paedophiles to it."

Once she had left, Anna said, "I am so, so sorry. You invite me to stay in your home to look after me and get rewarded with that spectacle. I am so embarrassed."

Mr Meeks not normally one to hold back said, "Anna, I already knew most of what was said, so please do not feel embarrassed. This is not just a dwelling place for recuperation; this is now your home, and I can assure you that woman will never ever be invited in again. You have to cut ties with her. She is nothing but poison. Next time we see her, she will be weeping and wailing for another reason: her partner in crime will be ordered to be imprisoned for a very long time."

They settled down to watch the film again, the atmosphere jaded by the toxicity that poisonous woman left behind. Mr Meeks said nothing for over an hour, then when the film was finished he said, "We need to tell the police about your mother. If she provokes you into reacting to her vicious tongue, you can be sure that she will use that against you and you will end up looking like someone who cannot control their temper."

Anna nodded because she knew only too well how manipulative her mother could be. "I think you are right. You have to be scraping the barrel if you are so taken in by a man who did what he did to me. At least we know where her loyalties lie."

Anna called the detective working on the case and told him what had happened. He said she could get a protection order which would mean her mother could not approach Anna again. Anna wasn't sure how effective this would be, but it was better than nothing, and at least this would add to the case against both her mother and her boyfriend.

Edwin was getting ready to go home. Both Mr Meeks and Anna would miss him. He too was reluctant to go. Mr Meeks made it clear that he was welcome back at any time, and he could bring his mother with him too. It would be lovely to catch up with her again.

When Edwin had gone, Anna said, "Did you mean it about Jenny coming to visit? Would that not be a bit awkward?"

"Oh, I think it would be extremely awkward, but I also think we are both old enough to manage that without coming to blows!" joked Mr Meeks.

Anna was settling into her new home, and Mr Meeks only really made contact when she requested it. They would share supper every other night, and he helped with all she couldn't do due to her arm, but even that was getting much stronger.

Edwin kept in contact with them, and a plan had been made for Edwin and Jenny to visit for a long weekend in a couple of weeks' time.

Anna received the documentation about the court date. She had not been looking forward to it but also felt once it was past, they could all get on with their lives.

Edwin asked if she would like him to be there for the court proceedings as support. Anna on one hand did not want to bother anyone but on the other she knew she would feel safer if Edwin was there. She called him back and asked if he would be able to take holidays for that time without any issue. He had said there would be no issue, and he could stay as long as she wanted him to – decision made.

Mr Meeks called Anna to say he had heard from Edwin, and he was coming that weekend and his stay would be indefinite. Anna felt a calm wash over her. Jenny would come with him the first weekend. Mr Meeks asked Anna if she would inspect the guest room to ensure it was fit for a lady coming to stay. Edwin had left some stuff in the room he had been using.

The other room was a little smaller but really bright as it had a large window and looked out onto the front of the house. It had a brand new bed which had never been slept in and some furniture, old fashioned but beautiful. Anna said with some nice bedding and a lamp it would be lovely. They opened the window to air the room and went out to buy some new bedding and bits and pieces.

Anna was looking at bedding with a very oriental look, which Mr Meeks thought really suited Anna. He looked at the price tag and knew there was no way she would buy it. Once the bedding and accessories were picked, he asked Anna to go to the food hall to buy a sandwich for them both and some juice.

He went to the till to pay for his goods after doubling back and picking up the boho bedding for Anna.

They drove to the beach to eat their lunch,

Mr Meeks said, "Anna what is your feelings on dogs?"

Anna said, "Dogs as in bow-wow dogs?"

Mr Meeks said, "Is there any other kind?"

They both laughed.

She said, "I have never owned a dog, but I have always wanted one. But don't worry I am not about to get one. I know that would drive you crazy."

Mr Meeks though for a moment, "On the contrary, I think you should get one."

Anna said, "Are you serious?"

"Absolutely serious. There is no better deterrent than a big dog."

Then the penny dropped for Anna: he was afraid for her and felt that if she had a dog, she would feel safer. The more she thought about it, the more she felt it might be a good idea.

Once they got home, Anna was making a salad for supper. She said, "I have thought about what you said about getting a dog, and I think you might be right. I did wonder about when I go back to work though, who would look after the dog then?"

"I would, of course. I have nothing more on daily."

Anna was surprised. She had not put the two together. *Mr Meeks and a dog? The mind boggles.*

Mr Meeks said, "It would have to be a biggish dog."

Anna said, "I was thinking a labradoodle."

Mr Meeks laughed, "Is that even a real thing?"

Anna collected her laptop and let him see the breed. She said, "The good thing about this breed is that they do not shed hair."

However, the cost was astronomical. Anna shut the laptop, feeling quite dejected, but not before Mr Meeks was able to take note of the website.

It was quickly approaching the weekend. Anna could tell Mr Meeks was really nervous. She had to admit she too was nervous. It was difficult to know how things would go; it had been a long time, and she did go off with his brother.

The day they arrived, Mr Meeks was running around like a headless chicken.

Anna said, "I mean this in the nicest way, but you have to bloody well calm down."

They heard the car draw up at the door. Anna opened the door and greeted them in her usual warm-hearted way. Mr Meeks behind her shook Jenny's hand.

Anna could see in an instant why Mr Meeks was so fond of Jenny. She was so unlike him, in fact almost opposites. She was, Anna thought, more like her.

It was a little awkward for about half an hour, and then the atmosphere softened and it became quite good fun.

Mr Meeks said, "Jenny, let me show you to your room and we can take your bags up. We usually have a movie night on a Friday, if you are up for that; the kids usually choose it."

"That would be great. Can I help with making supper or something?"

"We usually have a carry out so all you need to do is choose what you want from the menu. Oh, and put on your comfies, that's a must!"

When Jenny came back downstairs, she had on a pair of joggers and a t-shirt. She seemed surprised to see Mr Meeks in his comfies, so used she had been to seeing him in his formal gear.

She whispered to Anna, "I take it this is your influence."

Anna smiled and nodded.

"Well done you."

They enjoyed their evening. Anna went to bed around midnight, leaving Mr Meeks, Jenny and Edwin having a nightcap. As she was saying goodnight, she motioned to Edwin to go upstairs and let Mr Meeks and Jenny have some time together; they had things they needed to chat about. They were both looking relaxed, partly due to the alcohol they had had but also because they looked really comfortable in each other's company.

Edwin, not so naturally, jumped to his feet and said with a false yawn, "Well, that's it for me too."

Anna shook her head and had a little giggle to herself.

The following day, Mr Meeks and Edwin went out to get the shopping they required for the evening meal. Mr Meeks took the opportunity to ask Edwin for some assistance with looking for a puppy for Anna. Edwin said he might know someone who would be able to help. They had a lovely meal that evening, a curry made by Edwin, they played cards then scrabble, again having a few drinks. On Sunday morning, Anna had been sitting having a coffee looking out the window, and she heard a soft knock at her door. She went to the door. It was Edwin.

"Are you decent for visitors?"

Anna laughed. "Yes, sure. Coffee?"

"That would be lovely."

They chatted for a while, and Edwin asked Anna what she would do for a job once her arm was healed. The hospital had warned her against any heaving lifting so she would be limited to what she would be able to do.

"She sighed, that's a good question, Ed. I don't know."

He said, "I have a proposition for you. Would you give thought to working for me?"

Anna said, "I thank you from the bottom of my heart, but I wouldn't leave Mr Meeks now."

"What if I told you, you didn't have to move. In fact, you could work from home?"

"Doing what?"

"You know that I am an architect. Well, I have started my own business. I go and look at what is required with regard to plans, but I need someone to do all the business stuff and the appointments, and I am thinking of relocating here. Of course, I would need to speak Uncle Nigel to make sure he would be okay with me staying for a while until I can find premises."

Anna said, "Sounds fantastic, and yes, I would be interested, most definitely."

Mr Meeks knocked at the door. "Uh-oh. This looks like trouble. What are you two cooking up?"

Edwin said, "Well, there's no time like the present." He outlined his plan and asked that if possible could he stay with Mr Meeks for a short while, and he also explained all about offering Anna a job.

Mr Meeks could not hide his enthusiasm, and later that night, he said to Edwin that he had been having a think about the situation and offered him a place at the bottom of the garden to place an office. He also said to Edwin if he wanted to make his stay more permanent, he could use the attic. There was a room up there; it was converted and never used.

He took Edwin up to the attic. Edwin was gobsmacked. It was huge and would be perfect.

Edwin said, "We all have a great deal to think about. Let's convene again later in the day."

Mr Meeks went to speak to Anna. 'I believe Edwin has offered you work?"

"He has. It sounds like a good opportunity for me, a better job than I could get on my own."

Mr Meeks looked thoughtful, "What makes you say that?"

Anna said, "Oh, don't get me wrong. It's not that I think any job is too good for me or that I am not up to it, but with little in the way of qualifications and no experience, no one would even consider me."

Mr Meeks went on to tell Anna all about the plan for the office at the bottom of the garden and Edwin moving into the attic. Now she was looking thoughtful.

"You do know I only have your best interests at heart, don't you?" Anna said in a very adult teacher kind of way.

"Yes, of course!"

She continued, "Are you sure this is what you want? You have been so used to living in your own, and I think, but I could be wrong, you quite enjoyed the solitary life. Between me, the disco loving queen of loud music, and Edwin and his pernickety ways, don't you feel it might all be too much?"

Anna made a fair point, and he said as much, but he also explained it was years of being on his own that made him so set in his ways. He very much missed company, and the company he had chosen to mix with appeared to understand boundaries. He went on to say that the big old house had come alive since he met Anna and he felt as though his life once again had purpose and direction.

In true Anna style she said, "Well, what you waiting for, buddy? Let's get this show on the road."

He laughed.

Anna had not realised how lonely Mr Meeks was, but how could she? She hadn't known him when he was younger, and then the decision to give up work to look after his ailing parents changed everything.

That evening they had salad for supper, a picnic buffet, and they discussed the move. Mr Meeks had his reservations about Jenny being left on her own.

She said, "Well, actually, I was thinking of making a move too, it would be nice to come 'home' and I would like to be close to all you guys. I have been looking on the property register and there is a cottage at the other side of the wooded area at the back of the house for sale. I thought I might go have a look."

Mr Meeks house had a huge back garden which backed onto woods. The house had never been extended but that was not to say it couldn't be; they had never needed it before as there were so many rooms. He mentioned that as another possibility.

"Of course, the issue would be her selling her property," he said.

She smiled. "I rent my current property. When I finally sold Mum and Dad's, house, I wasn't sure what to do or where I wanted to settle, so I decided to rent for the foreseeable future to give me an idea of where I wanted to spend my remaining years."

"So there is nothing stopping this weird collection of people essentially living together," Anna described it beautifully. "This is fantastic," she raved. "I can't believe it. It's going to be like living in a commune."

They all saw the irony in that statement as each of them on their own merits were very independent people, they all thought for a moment and smiled. But that smile was also there to acknowledge that for many different reasons, they all actually needed one another.

Six months later and the office was built and in full operation at the bottom of the garden, the outside oak cladding making it look as if it had always been there. The attic was now home to Edwin. He arranged to have stairs outside the building so he did not have to use the front door of the house. Anna and Edwin both now had their independent access in and out of their space in the house, and Mr Meeks had his own front door back.

Jenny was still living in the house with Mr Meeks. The cottage had been sold to someone else. Mr Meeks said she should stay there until the perfect house came on the market. However, Mr Meeks and Edwin have a secret about the old cottage. They know the new owners… they ARE the owners.

They wanted to see how things would go with Jenny staying with Mr Meeks. He had said at the time he was not an easy man to live with as he had his odd way of doing things.

Edwin said, "I wouldn't worry about that too much. She lived with me and my way of doing things for long enough, and I am worried about her being on her own."

Edwin told Anna. She was not so sure about keeping this a secret. She explained to Edwin secrets have a way of coming out, and they can be misinterpreted causing hurt and mistrust.

Of course, Anna was right. The boys decided to come clean and did so over Sunday dinner. Jenny smiled as they were telling her, which was very confusing for them.

She said, "I have a secret of my own, boys… I know. I have always known!"

They all laughed, she continued, "So tell me, was it the baby of the group who said you should tell me?"

Edwin said, "Yes, how—?"

"You two are not as clever as you think. The mail coming to the house from the solicitors and the estate agents, the secret meeting to the solicitors. You would be no good in the secret service. 007's job is safe for now."

There was not such urgency for the puppy now that everyone was staying pretty much in the same place, but a promise is a promise.

Anna's birthday was coming up, and the puppies were to be a surprise for her... yes puppies. When Mr Meeks and Edwin went to visit them, there were only two left, one brown and one golden, so they took them both... never send a man on a mission of such importance.

The day of Anna's birthday, she woke to a funny sound. As she opened her eyes and adjusted to the light, she thought, *What on earth is that noise?* She sat up in bed and looked over by the window where the noise was coming from. She approached the big box pulling out the big red bow from the top and looked inside to find two Labrador puppies with *Happy Birthday* tags around their necks. Her other three housemates then burst into her room, with pressies galore. She felt so much like spoilt little princess.

She couldn't believe what they did that day, let alone the gifts they had. She got a Barbour jacket, Hunter Wellington boots, makeup, perfume, chocolates, but one gift from Mr Meeks completely blew her mind. She opened the envelope and it had lots of paperwork in it. She pulled it out still not sure of what it was. She began to read, but it was solicitor speak. She then came across something that looked like a certificate, it was only the deeds for the house.

She said, "I can't accept this!"

Mr Meeks said, "It's a little late for that. They are now in your name. There is a clause, however, that says you can't throw any of us out."

She laughed, "As if, who would make all my meals?"

Jenny said, "Speaking of meals, the birthday breakfast is served in the main dining room."

They put the puppies into their crates and went for breakfast. There was a bottle of champagne on the table in a bucket of ice. Mr Meeks stood to make a toast. They all toasted Anna a happy birthday.

Mr Meeks remained standing and said, "I have another announcement, which is in a way kind of a gift for you all. Well, I hope so anyway. Last night I asked Jenny to be my wife, and she accepted."

There was a moment of pure silence and then an almighty roar from both Anna and Edwin. They all hugged.

Anna said, "I too would like to say something. Mr Meeks and I met under the strangest of circumstances, and I know he has not shared the whole story with you to spare my blushes. However, he is the kindest nicest man I have ever known. He is so generous with his time and love, and I could not ask for a better more loyal friend. I am so pleased we met, and as Jenny says things happen for a reason. What's that saying again? 'What's for you won't go past you,' so true. Please raise your glasses to my new mum and dad."

Laughter could be heard from that room on a level never known before.

Mr Meeks suggested the puppies come through from Anna's so they could play with them. They were not allowed to go out for a walk as yet, but they could go out in the garden. Edwin had already arranged for someone to come the following week to puppy-proof part of the garden so the dogs could be out without fear of them being able to run off.

The little oddball family was working so well. They were all looking forward to Mr Meeks and Jenny's wedding; only a month to go. Edwin was best man and Anna bridesmaid. They hadn't really thought about inviting anyone else initially, so tight a unit they were in their little bubble, but one night Mr Meeks said, "We should probably think about sending out some invitations." The funny thing was they had ordered the big marque and disco but never actually thought about inviting anyone else.

Mr Meeks said, "We should probably ask the neighbours because they are going to have to keep up with the noise."

There weren't many, only another four houses in the street. They had all lived there for some time, so it's not like it would be new people.

Anna had a couple of friends she would like there, and Mr Meeks thought of a couple of people, the architect, his solicitor. Before they knew it, they were looking at nearly 100 people.

Anna said, "We are never going to be able to do the catering ourselves for that amount of people."

Edwin's girlfriend, Penny, was a chef so they asked her, and she was delighted to help out. This was going to be such a good day.

Two days before the wedding, dresses all altered to fit, Mr Meeks and Edwin wearing the traditional kilt. Catering organised (tick), disco booked (tick), cake ordered (tick), champagne ordered (tick), glasses rented (tick), porta-loo ordered (tick), hairdresser booked (tick), rings (tick)… they were all going over the list sitting at the dining room table.

Anna said, "Wouldn't it be funny if you had forgotten to book the most important person?"

They all laughed.

Jenny said, "What haven't we mentioned?"

Anna said, "Eh, the minister or humanist."

Mr Meeks and Jenny looked at one another and both shrugged.

Anna said, "Funny guys!"

Jenny said, "It certainly would be if it wasn't true."

Anna and Edwin said in unison, "No way!"

So the race was on. They had agreed on a humanist, but just hadn't done anything about it.

Anna said, "I know a woman that can do it, but she probably wouldn't be your choice."

Mr Meeks said, "Does she have two heads?"

Anna said, "No, but she has over 20 tattoos, blue hair and wears rings on her toes."

Jenny said, "More to the point, is she available?"

Anna said, "I can ask. You okay, Uncle Nigel?"

"Yes, yes, of course. Go phone, go phone quickly."

So as luck would have it "Magenta" was free and was delighted to be asked.

THE day arrived with much excitement in the house. Edwin took Mr Meeks out a long walk with the pups; the less time he was about the chaos the better. However, he had been incredibly laidback during the lead up and was going back to the uninhabited as yet cottage at the other side of the garden so he and Jenny did not lay eyes on one another before the ceremony. However, they turned up at Anna's.

She said to Edwin, "What's wrong?"

He said, "We rethought the whole walking over the soggy garden thing and decided to come here instead."

Edwin whispered, "Later!"

The ceremony was beautiful, they had made up their own vows and they were thoughtful and inspiring. Once the ceremony was over and they were sitting down to food, Mr Meeks stood to say his speech, which was quite funny. After all the speeches by Mr Meeks and Edwin, both Mr and Mrs Meeks stood up and asked Anna to join them. They handed her a large rolled-up poster.

Anna said, "I am a little scared at what this is. Better not be a photo of me with a face mask on."

She unrolled the poster, and it was a certificate of adoption. Mr and Mrs Meeks were "informally, because she as too old" adopting Anna. Inside the poster was also a form for her to complete a name change.

There was no way to stop what happened next, Anna threw herself into Mr Meeks arms and gave both Mr and Mrs Meeks the biggest happy tears, snotty hug they had ever had. Edwin and the pups, Bill and Ben, joined them. The photographer swooped in for what was to become their favourite photograph taken that day, the photo of their family, simple as that – no poses, no special effects other than their love for each other which was special enough to stand on its own.

It was a lovely day. The following day there were a couple of sore heads – not Anna though, she was still floating on cloud 9. She had texted Edwin to see if he fancied an early morning walk with the pups. He texted back: *If you can hang on 10 minutes, I will be down. I am rough though."*

They walked up into the woods. Once away from the house, Anna asked what had happened yesterday to make them change their minds about the cottage.

Edwin said, "Look, let's leave it for now as there is nothing we can do today."

Anna said, "Tell me, please. You are scaring me."

Edwin explained, "I went down to the cottage to take in a bottle for a wee dram before the ceremony and toiletries as we were going to get changed there; however, when I got there, the cottage was occupied."

Anna said, "Oh my God, what is it? Bats, rats, mice…?"

Edwin had to laugh a little at that, but he said, "No, people!"

She said, "People? What people?"

"Look, I don't want to upset you, and we can do something about this, so don't worry," Edwin replied.

She had stopped and was raising her voice, "Edwin, tell me!"

"It's your mother and some bloke!"

Anna handed the dog's leads to Edwin and stomped off. He was shouting after her but anger took over. Edwin began to follow as quickly as he could. The dogs hadn't clue what was going on.

Anna now practically running got to the cottage and thumped her fist on the door, again and again. Eventually, and just as Edwin had caught up with her, a guy opened the door. Anna barged past him, heading to the bedroom.

Edwin heard, "Get up you manipulating sick excuse for a parent."

Edwin arrived at the door in time to see Anna appear at the door with this very startled woman in a small silky nightdress who appeared to be struggling a little. Anna manhandled her to the door and shoved her out, went back in, closed the door and locked it.

This little fragile looking small woman with the silky number opened her mouth and suddenly she went from a timid looking OAP to some kind of wild animal; she was screaming at Anna. Edwin could see Anna through the bedroom window. She was filling black bags. As she filled one, it was getting launched out the window.

This woman shouted at Edwin, "For fuck's sake, don't just stand there, you pathetic little wanker. Do something!"

So he did. He let the dogs off their leads. They had been going mad barking and now they were right up at the couple barking. The guy said nothing the whole time. Their stuff was strewn all over the garden. The woman was frantically trying to find something to put on. She was swearing the whole time.

Anna came to one of the windows. "That's it all. Now get going, and I don't ever want to see you around here again."

They were now picking up their stuff and bundling it into a van.

She pointed at Anna, "You better watch your back, Missy"

Anna, said, "I have been having to do that since I was able to walk, you evil old bitch!"

Anna opened the door and let Edwin in. "I have decided I am moving in here, at least until Dad gets back."

Edwin laughed, "That sounds weird."

Anna said, "This is not funny, Edwin. If it had been anyone else, I would have said start paying rent, and I am sure we could think about it. But her, I cannot have her near me. She makes me want to vomit just seeing her."

They spent the rest of the day changing the bed and cleaning to the point of fumigation. Edwin went back to Anna's and took what she needed for that night. He knew she would be okay with the dogs there. They could think about what they were going to do the next day. Thankfully Mr and Mrs Meeks were on their honeymoon oblivious to it all, and Anna and Edwin agreed it should remain that way.

Edwin came over to the cottage for supper that night. He said to Anna, "Would you be happy to live here? I know it's not far, but it's not in the house, is it?"

She said, "I had already been thinking about it. I think they need some time on their own as newlyweds. They have never really had that, so I think I will make a complete move. It will be a surprise for them coming back."

Edward said, "I am not sure it will be a pleasant one, but for what it's worth, I think you are right."

They continued their evening, and the dogs settled into the cottage too.

The following day, Anna was afraid to leave the cottage until they had changed the locks. They called a locksmith who was able to come that day to do the work, and he fitted locks to all the windows too.

He said when finished, "No one will be able to get into the house without a code and the master key; that means you too if you forget the code or lose the key." He laughed. "But luckily you will always have your fingerprint."

It was pricy but so worth it. This way she had the confidence to leave the cottage knowing that that woman would not be able to get back in.

Edwin was moving some stuff out to put Anna's stuff in. He said, "Anna this drawer is full. Is it your stuff?"

She shouted from the other room, "No, I don't think so. Look inside. What is it?"

Edwin opened the drawer and had to sit down.

"Anna, I think you need to come see this."

Anna came through, in her head she was thinking, sex toys or something. But no, it was money, lots of money. They counted it, and it was around £100,000 give or take.

Edwin said, "Where the hell has this come from?"

Anna said, "Well, I can say with complete clarity, it's not mine."

Edwin said, "Would it belong to your mother?"

Anna laughed, "No!"

"Unless she is into something dodgy, which is entirely possible, I suppose," Edwin said. "You realise if it is hers, she will be back, and she might not be alone."

Edwin moved in with Anna. Days went past and still no sign of her mother or anyone else. They could not understand it.

Edwin said, "Did you look in any other drawers in that room?"

Anna replied, "No, I thought you did."

They trotted off to the smallest of the bedrooms, a room that had not been touched in years. It was basically as it had been when the previous owner left.

They opened the next drawer down to find a ledger. The total, however, was much more than they had found... until they opened the next drawer down.

Edwin said, "This looks as if this belongs to the last owner. We need to secure it until we find out how we get in touch with them."

Mr Meeks had a safe in is house, so they put it all in there for the time being.

They continued on with life forgetting about the stash in the safe, Anna moving into the cottage and Edwin now back at his place as he felt Anna was safe enough with the two dogs. They had had a call to say the newlyweds would be a few days longer as they were having such a good time.

Anna and Edwin, or Ed as he was now insisting she called him, wanted to surprise the newlyweds with a bit of a makeover of their sitting room. They had put a fresh lick of paint and bought some new seating, even just lightening the paint on the walls made such a difference. The seats were ordered a few weeks back, they were tartan, and they bought curtains in the same tartan, lifted the old carpet and sanded and varnished the wooden floorboards, and put down a neutral-coloured mat.

When they had finished, they were very pleased with their handiwork. Penny, Edwin's girlfriend, soon to be fiancé if she accepted – he was going to propose that weekend – went out shopping for some bits and pieces to add that polished effect.

Anna helped Ed to sort out the surprise for the proposal. It was a table in the woods, with a meal and champagne all decorated with fairy lights and flowers. Anna had to be there for the initial turn on of the fairy lights and then she left.

She got a text a couple of hours later to say, "She said yes."

Ed, unbeknown to anyone other than Anna at that time, had bought one of the houses in the village about a two-minute walk from them. Ed was worried they would be upset, but as Anna said it was two minutes away as opposed to miles or the other side of the world. He needed to do what was right for him and Penny. The house he had bought was their forever house. It needed some work but it had five bedrooms and a huge garden, not quite the size of Mr Meeks' place but pretty close.

The newlyweds called to say they were on their way home. Anna, Ed and Penny had everything ready. Penny had organised a beautiful picnic and Ed had put the gazebo up in the garden.

Mr and Mrs Meeks had been away much longer than they had intended, and they were about to surprise everyone with what they had been doing and where. The taxi door opened and out they came. They were barely recognisable, tanned and properly chilled.

"Welcome Home!" they all bellowed as they walked up the path. They had much more luggage than they left with.

Suddenly Anna twigged, "Where is your car?"

Mr Meeks said, "Well, that's a funny story. You know we were going to travel through the Highlands... well, that wasn't the plan. I had actually booked a holiday for us to visit India. I had heard Jenny say this was on her bucket list at some point, so I booked it, which means one of you guys will have to drive me to the airport, at some point, to pick up my car."

They walked into the sitting room and stood mouths open.

Anna, Ed and Penny shouted "Surprise! Happy wedding!"

Jenny said, "I love it; it is absolutely gorgeous. What a lovely surprise, guys. Thank you so much. Nigel, what do you think?"

"I think this room looks better than it ever has, between the decor and your lovely faces. What man could ask for more?"

They had lots of photos and stories to tell and lots of presents.

Jenny said, "Anna you would love it there. It is just your kind of place, so colourful and full of life."

Then they said, "So what's been happening here?"

They all looked at one another, and Ed said, "Well, we have had a bit of drama."

By the time Ed was finished, both Mr and, the new, Mrs Meeks were standing with their mouths open.

Mr Meeks went to speak, but Anna interrupted, "Ed..." She pointed at the photo.

He said, "Oh yes, sorry. There was something else. We found £200,000 in a drawer in the cottage. We have put it in your safe."

Mr Meeks said, "Well, Mrs Meeks, it would appear they have had a more eventful time than we have." He said in his usual manner, "Let's recap on some of these dramas. So Anna, you have decided to move to the cottage. If you are okay with that, then I am happy. Now that you have the dogs, you should be fine. So your mother was squatting in your new residence, but you got rid of her quickly enough. And Ed, you got engaged. Well, congratulations to you both. And you have bought a house, and you found £200,000. Have I mentioned everything?"

Ed said, "Yeh, I think that's about it."

The newlyweds laughed. They were so chilled that nothing appeared to be shocking them.

Mr Meeks said, "Edwin, let's go for a walk with the dogs. Leave the women to gossip."

Once out, Mr Meeks said, "Do you think our Anna is in danger from her mother and her associates?"

Edwin said, "Uncle, if you had seen her, I think it's her mother who may need to be careful."

"She is a lot more vulnerable than she lets on. So much hasn't happened to that wee girl."

"Thing is, Uncle, she wants her independence, but from what she was saying, she will never move very far."

"And you, Son, exactly how far away are you going?"

"Oh sorry, did we not say? You know old Mrs Baldwin's place?"

"What, on our street?"

"Yes. You didn't think I would move far, did you?"

"Where has Mrs Baldwin gone?" Mr Meeks enquired.

"She has moved into a home near where her daughter lives."

Jenny made a pot of tea.

"Are you okay after the altercation with your mother then?"

"Yes, I'm fine. It was a bit of a surprise, and the guy she is with looks as if he is so high, he hasn't a clue what's going on. I am surprised she hasn't come back; mind you, I am expecting her."

Jenny looked thoughtful. "Are you sure you feel comfortable enough in the cottage on your own?"

"I have the dogs, and I have my phone, and Ed insisted I install a pretty sophisticated entry and alarm system."

"I was just checking, and of course, if there are some nights you want to stay in the house, that's fine too."

Anna stood and hugged Jenny. "I have missed you."

The business was going well. Ed was looking to expand and hire another worker to do his side of the job. Anna was kept very busy with orders and booking job, etc., but loving every minute of it.

Ed said, "I have selected five candidates for the post. will you do the interview with me? I think you are better at reading people than I am."

Anna said, "You can go for two types of people – someone like you or someone the opposite of you – just depends on logistics after that I suppose. Do they live nearby? are they married?"

"What exactly do you mean by someone just like me?"

Anna laughed. "You know full well what I am referring to."

"I want to hear you say it, Miss People-watcher"

Anna said, "Okay, to be able to work together well, you need someone just as OCD as you or so much the other way that they are very laidback and nothing affects them."

Ed stuck his tongue out at Anna. "Such a clever clog, aren't you?" However, deep down, he knew she was right.

The interviews were arranged for the following week. On the day of the interviews, Anna wore her sharpest business suit, crisp white shirt and a pair of killer heels. When she walked into the office, Ed pretended he didn't know who she was. Anna spent most of her time in jeans and a t-shirt, and it wouldn't be the first time Ed had come into the office and Anna was was still in her pyjamas. It didn't matter as she wasn't seeing anyone; all her work was done on the computer.

Anna acknowledged his surprise and said, "Don't get used to it, buddy, it will be back to normal tomorrow."

The first four applicants, Anna questioned why they were even selected for the interview. The last one, though, Anna knew from the moment he arrived, he was THE one.

First of all, because the interviews were on a Sunday, he arrived in his jogging clothes. Apologising for the fact he was sweaty, he explained that he usually ran in this direction so he thought he could kill two birds with one stone.

Time management and good prioritising skills (tick). He had emailed his portfolio to Ed that morning instead of having to carry it, resourceful, (tick). His portfolio was brilliant (tick). And to round it all off, he was extremely easy on the eye (tick). His name: Joe. His age: 23. Marital status: single. *Thank you, God.*

When he left, Ed said, "Well, I think we are both agreed on that one."

"Absolutely! He is just the man for the job."

Ed said, "What!!!"

Anna replied, "He has everything you are looking for. He is very laidback, so your little ways won't faze him. He is clearly brilliant. You need to have another look through his portfolio."

Anna had also made up a points system for attributions required, and he topped the pole by a huge margin.

Once Ed had looked through his portfolio again, he realised this was the man for the job. Certainly he and Anna would get on because they were very similar.

Ed called him and said, "The job is yours if you want it."

He was delighted, and arrangements were made for a starting date there and then. He had just returned from travelling so had no job and was able to start straightaway.

He turned up that Monday with a pair of chino shorts and a t-shirt with a big smiley face on it, and a pair of flip flops. Anna had dressed well for the occasion; however, when she saw him, she breathed a sigh of relief and opted for her denim dungaree shorts and a white t-shirt.

He greeted her very warmly when she arrived. She apologised for not being there when he got there.

She joked, "It's not like I can say I had car trouble."

He looked at her, and he said, "You walk to work then?"

She was standing at the window. She turned to point to the cottage. "That's where I live."

He said, "Sweet, very handy."

She decided it was only fair that she explain their little family setup to avoid him putting his flip-flop clad foot in it at any point. When she had finished, he very sweetly said, "You guys have been lucky to find each other."

She knew then he would fit right in.

Joe was so easy to get along with. He did not give away much of himself though, and that made Anna suspicious. She had questioned him a few times on his past, and he had always deflected the questions, which of course made her more suspicious.

Joe was living in the attic at house A. He had been looking for a flat. but Uncle Nigel said it was no inconvenience to them and at least the space was being used. Anna was very well settled into the cottage. And what of the £200,000? Well, they tried to contact the previous tenant to be told she had passed away. The solicitor was trying to establish if she had any family but to date had not managed to come up with anything, They had decided if the money was to come back to them, they would donate half to the nursing home she had been living in.

Anna had no money worries these days and no stresses about very much really, apart from the court case against her mother's ex-boyfriend. Even once he had turned on her mother, she still would not believe he did what Anna had accused him of. As the date for court drew closer, Anna could feel her stress building.

Jenny came over for a coffee one Sunday afternoon. She asked how Anna was feeling about the court case.

Anna said, "Oh, I'm fine, be glad to see it over."

Jenny put her head to the side and looked Anna in the eye. "You are not fine, are you?"

Anna was about to protest and then thought what was the point, Jenny knew how worried she was. She began to get upset.

Jenny moved closer to her and took her in her arms. "It's all going to be fine. We will all be there with you."

Anna said, "That's part of what makes it so scary. You will all have to sit and listen to what he did, and I don't want that to have an influence on how we feel about each other."

Jenny said, "If you like, I can ask the boys to remain outside for that part. In fact, they don't need to come at all, but I will be there with you all the way."

"Do you think they would mind?" Anna questioned.

Jenny answered, "You know, I think they have been kind of expecting you to say this, and I also think there will be no argument on their part."

Anna looked relieved. "Will you tell them, Jenny?"

Jenny hugged her tight. "Of course, I will."

Ed's business was going from strength to strength, and he was thinking about taking on another employee. He also asked Anna if she wanted to do a business course at uni; not that she wasn't doing a fantastic job, but if she had the credentials to go along with it then she could opt to look elsewhere or use the qualification for something different.

Anna was overwhelmed by the offer and accepted immediately. She also told him that she had no intention of moving on and that she loved her job.

Ed said, "I thought you might say that, so I have had a good long talk to the boss."

Anna said, "Not good if you are speaking to yourself again."

He said, pretending to be annoyed, "Shut up you. I have decided to give you a promotion. You are now Business Manager, and along with that comes a hefty pay rise. Have a think about it and get back to me."

Anna said excitedly, "I will give it some thought. Yes, I accept."

They both laughed.

Anna said, "Wait a minute, what does this mean? What else will I be expected to do?"

Ed said, "Too late, you have accepted… seriously, I don't have time for the paperwork, any of it, so instead of taking on another architect, if you can deal with all the paperwork side and any client meetings, that would be fab."

Life was good, so good that Anna had stopped expecting the worst, until there was a knock on her door early one Sunday morning. The dogs were going mad, barking and running back and forth to the door. It was 5:30 am. Anna went cautiously to the door and looked out the spyhole. She could not see anything. Next thing she saw was the light of a torch. She had the phone in her hand ready to dial 999 when she realised Ed was the one holding the torch.

Anna opened the door. "What's wrong?"

At that moment, she thought it had been Ed who was knocking at the door. It turned out Ed set up one of those doorbell monitors which was why he knew someone was at the door. Anna chuckled a little to herself. He was so protective. She could have been annoyed as it was invading her privacy a little; however, she knew this came from a caring place, and right at that moment, she was grateful.

Ed greeted the dogs as they jumped the height of him in excitement. He said, "I'm pretty sure it was your mother at the door. I'm just not sure where she went."

Anna said, "My mother?"

Ed said, "She looked in bad state and possibly intoxicated. I am going to have a look around outside. I will take the dogs. They will find her if she is hiding."

Anna went back to the bedroom and put on a pair of joggers and a cosy jumper. She heard the dogs barking again, and her phone began to ring.

It was Ed. "Can you call an ambulance and come take the dogs? Your mother has collapsed. She is breathing but unconscious."

"Okay, be with you in a minute."

Anna called the ambulance and explained, giving all the info she had. She then grabbed her coat and followed the noise of the barking.

When Anna arrived at the scene, Ed had taken off his coat and laid it over her mother. Anna went up close. She staggered back in shock at what she saw. Her mother was barely recognisable. Her face was swollen almost beyond recognition, her nose had been bleeding, she had a large gash on her forehead and fresh and older bruising all over her body.

The ambulance arrived quickly. They checked for any neck or back trauma and loaded her into the ambulance.

Ed said, "We will get the dogs back to the house and follow in the car."

The paramedic asked them to bring any medication etc. Ed explained the circumstances.

Anna and Ed went back to the cottage with the dogs, and Mr Meeks arrived. He had heard the commotion and saw the blue flashing light of the ambulance. Ed went to put the kettle on.

Mr Meeks said to Anna, "You do not need to involve yourself in this if you don't want to."

Anna replied, "Yes, I know, but she looked so helpless lying there. I will do what I can just the same as I would do for any stranger."

This was more or less the answer Mr Meeks expected.

Ed said, "Uncle Nigel, why don't you go back to bed. I will take Anna to the hospital and wait with her until we establish what's what."

Mr Meeks quickly drank the rest of his cup of tea and stood. "If you are sure, I must admit going back into my cosy bed does sound appealing."

Ed said, "We will be fine. I will take good care of her."

Teapot now drained dry, Anna and Ed headed to the hospital. They were advised the doctor would come to speak with them when he had finished examining Anna's mother.

About 20 minutes later, the doctor in charge of A&E knocked on the door. "Excuse me, are you Anna and Ed?"

"We are," Ed answered.

"My name is Dr Marshall, and I am in charge of the A&E unit tonight. I am so sorry to have to pass on the news that

Mrs Downie passed away shortly after arriving at A&E. She was found to have a large contusion on her head and bruising all over her body. I can take you to see her if you like, and the police will also want to speak to you before you leave."

They passed on all the information they currently had. Anna advised she did not really have a relationship with her mother and hadn't had for some years. The police asked if either of them had any idea of who may have caused the injuries. Anna was able to give a couple of names from the past but felt it was more likely to be the guy she was living with; she had heard he had a history of domestic abuse.

Anna felt awful, she was having a really hard time having any feelings at all about the situation. She felt so removed from her biological family. They made their way home, and Anna went straight to the cottage.

Jenny knew this must have been very upsetting for Anna. Regardless of their current relationship, she was still her mother. She texted Anna: *"Kettle's on!"*

Anna replied, *"Two minutes."*

Jenny felt comfortable speaking about most things with Anna, and was more direct nowadays than she had been, so she went straight for it. "Anna, I feel I have to say something. I can see you tearing yourself apart thinking that you should be more upset about your mother, and you feel bad not being able to cry. She made a choice many years ago, a choice you or I would never consider: she chose a man over her own child. She is virtually a stranger to you, and considering how she treated you, you really have nothing to reproach yourself about."

Anna said, "I know, but she looked so tiny and vulnerable, not to mention how badly she was beaten."

Jenny said, "I think your mother did the best she could, and holding any grudge or anger about that isn't helpful to anyone. She continually chose the wrong kind of men and seemed oblivious to the fact that was an issue. However, the fact she headed to you when she needed someone says a lot, don't you think?"

Anna nodded. "I suppose so."

Jenny continued, "You can break the cycle, Anna. You can make your life so much better, and even if she didn't say it, I am sure that is exactly what she would want for you."

Anna said, "You always have a way of making me feel better. I'm so glad I have you in my life."

Jenny wiped a tear from her cheek, put her arm around Anna and hugged tight.

The funeral took place the following day. It was sad, and Anna did have a cry. The ex-boyfriend had the nerve to show up despite being investigated for the assault. He stood behind and asked Anna if he could speak to her. Anna nodded. Jenny also remained behind.

He introduced himself as Mike. He wanted them to know he had nothing to do with what happened. He told her that the guy she had left him for had got her hooked on heroin, and he felt he may be the perpetrator. He was well known for being violent. He supplied drugs all over the city, and people were too scared not to pay up.

Anna thought about this and said to Jenny, "I think he may be telling the truth, you know. It would be just like my mother to get involved with that. She had a very addictive personality."

Mike had been able to give her a name so she decided to have a look online to see if she could get any further info on him.

They all went back to Whitford Grange for a cup of tea and a buffet. A woman approached Anna. She felt this woman was familiar but didn't know who she was.

The woman said, "You don't recognise me, do you?"

Anna said, "You look familiar, but I'm sorry, I can't place you."

She began, "I'm Stella, your mum's best friend."

Jenny put a protective arm around Anna.

"That's right. Sorry, it's been a while. How are you? You are looking well."

Stella laughed, "Well, I must be looking better than the last time you saw me. I was in quite a mess, but I have been clean for five years. I have been through detox and a lot of counselling to get to where I am today. This must have been quite a shock for you. I know you and your mum didn't get on that well but that was down to the junk."

Anna looked wistful. "I don't think Sylvia ever wanted to be a mother. I wasn't in regular contact with her. She chose that idiot she was living with over me. After what he did to me, there really was no going back."

"I know who you are talking about. He is NOT a nice man. Do you think he had anything to do with what happened to your mum?"

"Well, he hasn't been seen since, so I imagine if he didn't do it, he knows who did"

"Are the police looking for him?"

Anna laughed, "Yes, they are, but they also seem to have me down as a suspect too."

Stella left her telephone number with Anna. She asked her to call should she need someone to speak to.

Anna was grateful for the offer, but she had people in her life she could trust, people she knew had her back no matter what.

The following day Anna felt wave of relief that the funeral was over. The toast made its announcement that it was ready to eat with a loud accomplished pop from the toaster. When she heard the doorbell, she wasn't even dressed.

When she opened the door, two policemen were standing there. They reluctantly explained that they had to take her to the station for further questioning. She knew this was down to DI Jamieson. She seemed determined to prove Anna had something to do with her mother's untimely passing. They allowed Anna to get dressed before heading to the station.

Once at the station, she waited well over three hours before DI Jamieson made an appearance. She was trying to rattle her, waiting for her to make a mistake so she could throw the book at her.

Anna could read her like a book. She had seen enough police programmes to know how this type of intimidation worked, but she was barking up the wrong tree. Anna had nothing to do with this. She had a lot of resentment towards her mother, but it was never strong enough for her to do something like this. It seemed obvious to everyone apart from DI Jamieson that her mother's now missing boyfriend was the real culprit.

Anna was questioned at length again – the same questions, the same allegations and the same answers. DI Jamieson never seemed happy with the answers Anna gave; however, she couldn't change them because they were actually the truth. Anna was returned to her cell and eventually let go.

The following day when Ed came into the office he asked, "Where were you last night? Penny and I popped round and the cottage was in darkness."

"I was at my alternative address, the police station, being questioned, yet again"

Ed was not best pleased. "We need to get a solicitor. This is complete harassment. I have no idea what she thinks she is hoping to find. Leave it with me; I have a friend who is a solicitor. I will get some advice on how to proceed with this. I feel we have enough information to lodge a complaint. She's determined, I will say that for her. Don't worry about it, once they find the real culprit, she will leave you alone. They are grasping at straws; however, until they find him, she will continue going after you, so I think from now on you should not be questioned without a solicitor."

Anna knew what he was saying made sense, but she still had faith in the system, and knew she was innocent, so it was impossible for them to have anything on her. That didn't stop DI Jamieson from pushing, and pushing. She said now that Anna had hired a solicitor, it meant she had something to hide. Anna had been advised to say nothing.

"No comment to every question."

The police were making heavy work of finding their person of interest. Anna thought this strange as from what she knew of him, he was not the smartest tool in the box, so how was he managing to evade the police at every turn?

The two policemen were becoming restless the longer she took to get dressed and get her things together. She tried to hurry things along, and before long, she was being helped into the police car. That always intrigued her. Human beings get in and out of cars all the time, so why would they suddenly need help to get into a car just because it's a police car. On arrival at the station, she was formally charged and her fingerprints taken, and she was taken to a cell.

Ed called the solicitor, frantic. "Richard, she has been arrested, not just taken in for questioning. They read her her rights."

"Right Ed, I will get down there, don't worry. This is just showing how desperate they are. They have nothing."

Ed scratched his head. "They are saying they have found her fingerprints in the house."

"That's okay though because she would have lived there at one time, wouldn't she?"

"No, that's the thing. She has never been in that house. The last time she was in a house with her mother, it was her old house on Abington Way, that's where this brute attacked Anna."

Richard looked a little confused. "He attacked her? When was this?"

"Oh, some time ago now. We think, although it was never proved, that he had someone follow her to her flat to attack her too. This was when she ended up staying with Uncle Nigel."

"Was this reported to the police at the time?"

"Yes, but they couldn't find any proof of it being organised by Ely, and the charges were dropped."

"This is fantastic news. It's interesting that this has never actually come up in the course of this investigation. Leave this with me. DI Jamieson has been lighting little fires all over the place, and it would seem she is just about to catch fire herself.”

Mr Meeks, Jenny, Edwin and Penny sat nervously waiting for news. They heard the front door open and they stared expectedly at the lounge door, all expecting it to be Richard with bad news. When Anna burst in, they all rose to their feet and hugged.

Ed grabbed Richard’s hand and shook it vigorously. “Thank you so much, Richard. I cannot find the words to tell you how happy we are. We have become a proper little family here, and the thought of it breaking up would just kill us all.”

“You are most welcome. The case against DI Jamieson is picking up pace, and she will most likely serve time and will never return to her job. DS Jones has also been suspended because she has had to know about what was happening. Ely is now in custody, and the investigation will start again. It’s not looking good for him; he has a long history of domestic abuse.”

They ordered a pizza and cracked open a few bottles of wine.

Jenny said to Anna, “Remember, Anna, when all is said and done, this woman was still your mother, and it’s okay to feel bad for her and yourself.”

“I’m fine, Jenny; however, I do have to go clean out her house and get it on the market.”

“She bought that property?”

“Yes, apparently she had a win on the lottery and bought the house then.”

“Well, we will all come help when you decide to do the clear out, although, we better not leave it too long as she is bound to have had food in the fridge. Perhaps we can go do that tomorrow.”

“Unfortunately, we can’t get in as yet. It’s all still taped off as they are continuing with the investigation, but they said they would call when we can get access.”

They all went off to bed that night with a smile on their faces. Anna couldn’t wait to tell Joe all about it. Joe had basically been holding down all the day-to-day work on his own.

The following morning Anna woke early. She sat out on the patio to eat her breakfast, and she finally felt the relief she hadn’t been allowing herself to feel in case it all went wrong. She heard someone whistling. It was Joe.

“You’re an early bird today!”

“I couldn’t wait to see you to congratulate you. I have been so worried about you all. It must have been awful.”

Anna went to speak, but he interrupted.

“New rule: this is the last time we are going to mention it. Let’s have a sensational day, well, days, starting by you getting dressed, not for work though, for play. We are off on an adventure. Oh, and pack a bag for a couple of nights.”

She received a text from Ed: *Have a ball, little one.*

She thought, *Do I have the best family or what?*

They set off and headed north.

“Where are we going?” Anna asked excitedly.

“It’s a secret for now, but I’m sure you will guess before long.”

The further they drove, she knew where they we going, Callan, a place she had been when she was young her with her

Aunt and Uncle. They had a caravan there, and she spent a few weekends there.

She squealed in delight as they approached the sign for the village; however, they went straight past the caravan site.

"Now I'm a little confused, or you are lost?"

"Nope, not lost, just wait and see."

They headed through the village and towards the beach. There were a few cottages that looked out onto the sea. In fact, you had direct access to the beach from them. She felt a shiver of excitement as they drew up alongside one of the cottages.

She said in a tone way higher than her normal voice, "You have never managed to rent us this for the weekend?"

"No, sorry, I haven't. We've only gone and bought it!!!"

"Bought it? I don't understand. Who's bought it?"

"We. Well, technically, you have bought it."

They were still sitting in the car.

"You want to go in, or are we just going to sit here and look at it?"

Joe handed Anna the key. She jumped out and still half expected it to be a joke and the key wouldn't fit, but no, it did unlock the lock. The door creaked open, and she ran inside.

Inside was in need of some decoration, but it was clean and dry, and that view, breathtaking. There was still furniture in the cottage. Anna pulled the dust covers off the sofa and sat down.

"Okay, Joe, explain this to me. How did I, Anna Meeks, with very little money in the bank manage to buy this property, and how much are the repayments going to be each month? Hopefully, someone has looked at that to see if I can afford it or not?"

"No repayments, Ms Meeks, you bought it outright."

"How?"

"Cast your mind back a few months. Remember the £200,000?"

Anna nodded, then what he was saying registered in her brain.

"Oh, my God, you never used that?"

"It's okay. It's all above board. The solicitor put out a search for the previous owner, and it appears she died and had no family. However, the argument would have been how they would have been able to prove the money was theirs because we don't actually know that for sure. So it meant that it came back to us. It all happened so quickly, but the cottage came on the market, Mr Meeks saw it, and him and Ed put in an offer that day."

Anna was grinning from ear to ear. "Seriously things could not be better, really could not be any better. This is the stuff dreams are made of, and all this started off in such an unlikely manner."

Anna turned to look out the window at the incredible view before her. When she turned back to speak to Joe, he was kneeling on the floor. She was just about to ask what he was doing when he produced an engagement ring.

"I have never known anyone quite like you, Anna Meeks, and from that first day we met, I knew we were destined to be together forever. Being with someone forever had never been in my plans until then, but sometimes life has a way of changing those plans. I love your spontaneity, your love for life, your total connection and commitment to family, the fact that your family setup is weird but you are so proud of that. I love your laugh. I love when you pretend to get into a bad mood with the dogs when they have been misbehaving but end up laughing anyway. I don't know why or how but we work. We work so well so I would like to ask you a question: will you be my wife?"

Anna was crying and laughing at the same time. "Yes, yes, yes, of course, I will."

At that moment, the door burst open and "the family" rushed in with champagne, balloons, a cake and lots of hugs and congratulations.

Uncle Nigel made a toast and told Anna how Joe kept with tradition and had come to ask his permission to ask her to marry him, and how he not only had given his permission but was delighted for them both. He saw the way Anna looked at Joe. She was never going to turn him down; they were made for each other.

They weren't planning a wedding anytime soon. They wanted to spread their wings a little, and although Mr Meeks was saying all the right things, he did confess to Jenny after that he would have preferred for Anna's reputation that they made their relationship official.

Jenny laughed. "My dear Nigel, that bit of paper does not guarantee happiness, or loyalty for that matter, only feelings and commitment can do that, and they have that in abundance. Anna is so young, but all she has been through has made her grow up faster than she should have had to. I think she needs a bit of adventure especially as she knows she has a home and people who care about her to come back to."

"What did I do to deserve you back in my life, Mrs Meeks? I can't remember who said it but someone said in a film, 'You complete me.' That's exactly what I feel you have done for me. You complete me."

"Nigel, that's a lovely thing to say. It was Jerry McGuire."

"Who?"

Jenny laughed, "Never mind."

These seven people found one another under some extraordinary circumstances. Some may call it fate, while others may feel there have been stronger forces at work depending on your own beliefs, but there is no question that the only person out of the whole scenario that did not benefit from these cosmic forces was Edward, however influential he was in bringing everyone together. That was maybe his penance for some of the more underhand things he had done in the past.

There is a great saying that goes: "Friends are the family we choose." In this instance, family is what this group of people found when they needed a friend.